THORNBERRY ANIMAL SANCTUARY'S

BOOK OF SHORT STORIES 2020

ONCE UPON A TIME THERE WAS A CAT AND A DOG

First published 2020 by Thornberry Animal Sanctuary.

Front and back cover by Lindsay Hewson

Thornberry Animal Sanctuary

Charity Number: 1018048

www.thornberryanimalsanctuary.org

info@thornberryanimalsanctuary.org

Telephone: 01909 564399

Address: Thornberry Animal Sanctuary, The Stables, Todwick Road, North Anston, S25 3SE

Thornberry Animal Sanctuary is a well-established animal rescue centre that has been operating in South Yorkshire for over 31 years. We are one of the largest animal rescue charities in the area, being able to house over 100 animals at any one time. We care for equines, farm animals, dogs, cats, rabbits and other small animals. As of May 2020, we have 27 staff and an army of volunteers. In the last 12 months, we rescued and rehomed 173 dogs, 189 cats and kittens, 125 small animals including rabbits, 56 equines and over 3000 hens.

FOREWORD

In April 2020, when so many people were living in restricted or completely isolated circumstances, we decided to run a story-writing competition. We hoped to provide an interesting and diverting activity, maybe even a challenging one, which would invite writers of all ages to reflect on the place of domestic animals in our world.

You, the writers, rose to the challenge, with 120 stories presented here!

The suggested starting point for each story was: 'There was a cat and a dog….' From that point on, however, the similarity ends. The collection shows a creative explosion of different treatments of that theme, of different styles, viewpoints and emotions. What they do share, however, is an underlying compassion for the lot of many a pet in the human world and a desire to make it better. Clear-sighted realism and wisdom were also shown by many, even amongst the very youngest writers here.

I thoroughly enjoyed reading each story. The task of judging, however, was harder; there were so many worthy contenders. I had the help throughout of an excellent and stalwart co-judge, Sue McNeela, who helped to choose the winner and runner-up for each of the age-groups. Huge thanks go to her. We were strict on the word count of 250 for judging but have been happy to include longer stories in the book.

We hope you enjoy the stories and also that collectively, we have made the world a little bit better for our animals, and in doing so, also for ourselves.

Jane Sara (Trustee: Thornberry Animal Sanctuary)

WINNERS & RUNNERS-UP

AGE GROUP WINNERS

3-7 years old

Winner: Eva Royston
Runner-up: Matilda Mellon

8-10 years old

Winner: Noah Mullins
Runner-up: Alice Parke

11-15 years old

Winner: Keira Boulton
Runner-up: Sadie Roberts

Adult group

Winner: Rhianna Bonsall
Runner-up: Adam Morris

ONCE UPON A TIME THERE WAS A CAT AND A DOG...

WINNER
Eva Royston, 5 years old

Once upon a time there was a dog named Humphrey and a cat named Kiki who lived with a little girl called Eva. Eva wanted to be a poet. She practiced her poetry every day. She read her poems to her audiences, which were Humphrey and Kiki. They usually just yawned and fell asleep which made Eva thinks her poems were boring. She always used everything she saw as inspiration to write a poem. This could be food, the outdoors, bath time, bedtime, even just sitting on the sofa. One day Eva decided to write a poem about her dog and cat.

Kiki and Humphrey sleep all day,
When they are awake all they do is play,
They eat food and treats,
Sometimes they even steal our meats,
Kiki stays indoors,
Humphrey goes outside,
Usually they like to be side by side,
I love my dog and cat,
My dog and cat love me,
Together we are a family.

Eva read this to Humphrey and Kiki but instead of falling asleep their ears pricked up and they seemed to listen for the first time ever. After she read her poem to them they ran up to Eva and cuddled and licked her. This made Eva really really happy. She knew this poem wasn't boring at all.

She continued to write poetry daily and when she grew up she became a famous poet, and she even read her poems to the Queen. She always read to Humphrey and Kiki first for approval though. They would always be her best audience.

THE END

RUNNER-UP
Matilda Mellon, 6 years old

Once upon a time there was a Cat and a Dog. The Dog was called Ralph. He was black with pointy ears. The Cat was called Selwin. He was black and white and very fluffy. They were best friends and they went to the park together At the park they saw a Unicorn on the slide and a big Tiger on the swings. The Tiger Roared at Ralph and made him jump with joy.

Now I know you are thinking that the roar might have hurt Ralph's ears, but it didn't.....Ralph wanted to play!

Selwin went to play with the tiger and admired his stripes. Ralph went to play with the Unicorn and all of the animals had a big party. They even had a rainbow cake! At the end of the party everyone was tired. They all went home to their owners.

But did you know that every so often they have a secret meet up? It is a disco party! The next time you go to the park, look out for the Cat, the Dog, the Unicorn and the Tiger having a party!

WINNER
Noah Mullins, 9 years old

They happened to meet and didn't know anything about each other. "What is your name?" asked Mr. Dog. The cat replied with his nose stuck in the air, "My name is Monsieur Chat. Why are you asking me this question?"

"I...I only wanted to play with you," stammered Mr. Dog.

"Why would I want to play with you? We have nothing in common," announced

Monsieur Chat. "Do you like to play with a ball?" questioned the dog. "Yes" said

Monsieur Chat. "Do you like to stay in a warm cozy home?"

"Yes" said Monsieur Chat. "Do you like to eat yummy food?"

"Oui," said Monsieur Chat. "Ok, 1 love all these things too," explained Mr. Dog.

"So now do you want to play with me?"

"Splendid!" exclaimed Monsieur Chat "What do you want to play first?"

"Just because we don't look the same doesn't mean that we can't be best of friends," explained Mr. Dog later that day. "You are very wise Mon Ami," agreed Monsieur Chat.

RUNNER-UP
Alice Parke, 10 years old

The desert sprawled across the parched land, baked by the sunshine. Hidden under a rock in the shade, the only escape from the immense heat, was a tribe of tired- looking cats and dogs. There were stripy cats and black dogs all bundled up in a close huddle. This was an unusual tribe because wild cats and dogs are normally enemies but this group worked as a team.

As the sun thumped down on the arid desert floor, the meekest of the cats started to abruptly fidget. She peeped round the jagged corner of the rock and jumped at the sight of a mighty eagle soaring through the sky, circling above their stash of food (an antelope which they'd worked hard to catch). The cat yelped and the rest of the tribe woke up with a start. Just as they got to where the cat was standing, the greedy bird pounced on their prey and swooped up into the sky.

The cats whisked up into the tree and dived to reach the eagle's scraggy tail. Ten cats hung from the bird, like the tail of a kite. As they lunged through the sky, the eagle started to lose control and its grip of the antelope. The dogs got into position and caught the falling antelope, passing it to each other like a rugby ball.

The eagle plunged into a gigantic sand dune. The supportive team came together and greedily ate their supper before falling back to sleep in their huddle again.

WINNER
Keira Boulton, 15 years old

Preconceptions. A subconscious way of thinking.

It started with a couple who became owners to a cat and dog, more specifically, a bashful, brown-furred puppy and a delicate, white kitten. They grew up together, were raised almost identically. The animals taught each other their characteristics. Eventually the two wonderful worlds merged together, making them the perfect pair. People's opinions never changing though. The puppy acted too much like a kitten and vice versa.

The day it happened, the duo were on the front garden, doing their usual routinely walk when the kitten spotted a mountain of bricks piled up. Curiously, he started to climb, step by step, looking back expectantly at his friend still on the ground. The puppy was dubious at first, before deciding to follow along but clumsily pushed the bricks off the pile as he made his way up, making it impossible to go back down.

Once the two had noticed this they panicked, but the kitten elegantly jumped down, making a perfect land. However this was not too easy for the dog. The owners, who were sat outside, noticed this and worried, realising the pile was too tall for them to get the whimpering puppy. What could they do?

But to everyone's surprise, even the puppy's, with trembling arms he jumped. The owners' eyes widened as they watched, rushing to the falling puppy. However, the small pet made a land on its paws, almost too easily.

Then they realised, cats always land on their feet.

RUNNER UP
Sadie Roberts, 11 years old

A bullmastiff, Champ, was a guard dog for a small family. One day, while basking in the sunlight on the stone tiles in the garden he saw a group of boys by the river opposite his house. He readied to chase them away if they neared his family. To his surprise, they held a basket, that was SQUEAKING?! He knew that was not right and decided to take action.

He jumped over the large fence and rushed towards the river, sending the boys scattering. Without hesitation, he dived into the river to retrieve the basket. As he placed it on the bank, he noticed something struggling to get out. He gently tipped over the basket and a small, black and white kitten tumbled out, her fur matted and soaked. "Come with me" Champ said, "I know somewhere you will be safe"

He took the young kitten, whose name was found to be Nala, on a long, harrowing journey but carried and protected her the whole way. After many days and nights of travelling, they reached their destination. As Nala looked up with her brown eyes, she saw a sign that read, 'Thornberry Animal Sanctuary.' She didn't know what 'Sanctuary' meant, but it made her feel safe. "Wait here," Champ whispered as he pressed the doorbell. And with that, he continued on his journey home, comforted by the thought that his little friend was now in a place filled with love and happiness.

The End

WINNER
Rhianna Bonsall

Safe

I don't have a name, although sometimes they call me Lexi. But only when they drag me before other humans, in their warm room with the soft ground, smiles baring their teeth. Otherwise, the only attention I get is a kick to the face when they plonk a bowl of mouldy kibble in my cage. That is, if I'm lucky. Most of the time, I go without both.

I am sore. My teats are still pink and distended, reaching out for little mouths to grasp on to them. But the little mouths are gone again, the pups they belong to sold to human mothers. Just as they always are. They are gone, but I remember them. I remember them all.

The cage door rattles, and I cower in my soiled corner, barricading myself from the descending avalanche. What will it be this time; a kick, my reward of stagnant water? A stud, cowering like me, delivered to bring yet more babies into the world through this squalor?

But the face of the human is one I haven't seen before. She reaches out her arms and removes me from the filth. I flinch as her hand comes to my face, but it trails my fur with a gentle touch, making me tingle. My tail wags involuntarily.

"Don't worry girl, you're safe now."

Safe. I've never heard that word before, but I think I'm going to like it.

RUNNER-UP
Adam Morris

My name is Lola. I'm six weeks old. I'm a good girl. I like to wag my tail when I'm happy. I go woof a lot. I have cream fur. They have specs of creme-brulee on the tips. My tail is a fluffy cloud. I like to play with other dogs and hoomans. I really REALLY like walkies.

My name is Lola. I'm three months old. I'm a good girl. I go woof a lot. My first hoomans didn't like that very much. It was too loud. They used to punish me...

My favourite place to hide is under a chair. I'm great at being outside. Even if it's wet. Even when my nose is sore from sniffing snow. Even with the twister of sticky mud and sharp sticks tangling into my fur.

My name is Lola. I'm five months old. I go woof a lot. I like to play with other hoomans. My second hoomans were good at that. Their littlest hooman was really good at that.

One day the little hooman stopped breathing. He went to a place where poorly hoomans live. They said he couldn't breathe. They said my fluffy fur was the problem. My tail is a fluffy cloud. I didn't mean to.

I had to live in a room all by myself. I'm good at being alone.

My name is Lola. I'm six months old. I go woof a lot. Am I good girl?

WITH A SPECIAL MENTION FOR THE FOLLOWING STORIES

Evie Peers, 7 years old

This story is about a secret club held by a cat called Heather and a dog named Betty. Betty is a purple sparkly poodle with a bow in her hair. Heather is a cat with short hair and a long neck. She is white all over.

Betty just wants to have fun, whilst Heather likes investigating mysteries but they have one thing in common; they are both really playful. The secret club is held in the basement of Betty's house.

One day they were in the basement and Heather cried, "My owner said we have to move house to Africa!!!" There was silence then Betty shuddered, "What should we do?" They were extremely worried that they will not be able to carry on with the club.

They thought and thought of what they could do, then Heather burst out, "How about we go to my house and see exactly where I am moving?" They went to Heather's house and saw on the kitchen table there was a map and, on that map, there was a cross and it said Africa Lane. So Heather was not moving to the continent of Africa, she was moving to Africa Lane, which was only a few streets away. They could carry on with their secret club!!!!!!!!!!!!!!!!!!!!!!!!!!!!!!!

They felt relieved and excited because of all of the plans they have got for their secret club. They went off to solve the mystery of the book who walked away…

Siddhi Tammewar, 8 years old

Once upon a time there was a cat and a dog called Lucy!

I, Siddhi, always dreamt of having a pet dog and eventually it came true on one special day…on my birthday! My best gift ever! My parents let me pick her name because it was my special birthday gift. I named her Lucy.

She became my best friend. I take her for walks in our estate and we would play games like: fetch, throw and catch and many more. My little sister and Lucy used to play together when I am at school. I and my little sister always loved to play with her and she loved us too.

One afternoon, I and my sister were painting in our playroom and Lucy was running around but after some time…she disappeared. I was so scared I looked everywhere in the house but I couldn't find her; mum and dad were looking for Lucy too but no luck. I was very sad. I didn't want to lose my dream dog that I've always wanted for a long time.

We checked the back and front yard but she wasn't there either. We were puzzled. We walked around the estate to see if she went away for a walk but couldn't find her anywhere.

I burst into tears. I just wanted Lucy back!!! I made a 'missing' note with Lucy's picture and distributed it in the estate.

I am sure My Dream Dog will find her way back to me and then I will never let her go away.

Tyler Roper-Dewey, 8 years old

Once upon a time there was a cat and a dog and they lived in Thornberry Animal Sanctuary with some other animal friends. There was a horse a rabbit and 2 Guinea pigs and they were all best friends.

At night when all the humans had gone home, they had a party and invited all the other animals to come. They had to try and be quiet so nobody would hear them. They had a pile of Carrots and Apples and Hay that they had stolen from the humans in the day so they could eat them all together and laugh and play. They also had music like a disco and danced all night.

The friends would plan every day to steal the food and hide it somewhere safe. They had rat friends that helped them as they are small and they can run fast.

They had to make sure they cleaned up and put everything away before the humans came back in the morning so no one would know.

All the Animals are very happy and look forward to their party each night so they can relax and dance together and have lots of fun.

The End

Kayla-Jade Roddis, 11 years old

Once upon a time there was a cat and a dog. Both of them had abnormal features such as the dog had such long legs that he was practically the size of a house; the cat, on the other hand, had ears the size of an A3 piece of paper! Neither of them had been accepted into families and were put into a pet centre. It was falling to pieces and smelt of damp. There, the two of them met.

They decided to escape through a small gap in the wall leading to an alleyway. Then (with their astonishing features) decided to work together. The massive ears and long legs were a perfect match. Together, they travelled far and wide to find a place that they could call home. They lived in peace and harmony for the rest of their existence.

Jessica Lewington, 11 years old

In Rogerstone there was a RSPCA centre with many animals, but two of them were special, a black and white collie puppy called Harvey and a ginger kitten called Willow. They were best friends that stuck together even in the most dangerous of situations. They had saved each other multiple times, but once they were both in trouble and got rescued by the RSPCA and were separated. It was years later that they were adopted. Harvey was adopted by a family with two children, Alfie and Amy, who were kind and loving. Willow was adopted by a caring old woman called Mrs Jones.

Harvey was scared that he would never see Willow again. Amy and Alfie struggled to get Harvey out of the shelter, because all he wanted was to be with Willow, to keep her warm and safe but he gave up; he would never see his best friend again.

Willow felt alone. Her only friend had been taken away; who would keep her warm at night, who would keep her safe?

But it turns out Mrs Jones was Alfie and Amy's Grandma.

Alfie and Amy took care of their Grandma very well. Some of the time they would bring Harvey with them so he could play in the garden with Willow for hours until it was time to go home. At last the furry friends are reunited for many days to come.

Evie Betts

Once upon a time, there was a cat and a dog. They lived in the same house and they were as close as two best friends could be. Who knew that one day the two of them would experience a life changing event? One sunny day, their owner (Mrs Bramley) came home from work as she normally did,carrying a large box. Bending down, she Lovingly gave the cat a tickle behind the ear and the dog a pat onhis head. Next, she went into the living room and carefully put the box on the floor before hanging her coat up. Excitedly she opened the mysterious looking box that she had previously put down. Slowly, she reached into the box and pulled out not one but three tiny kittens! She put them on the floor and then she went back out to the car and walked in with another mysterious looking box. This time she pulled out three puppies. The cat and the dog sat there in shock, gazing at the tiny kittens and puppies in amazement. Up to this point, the dog and the cat had had a very peaceful life until Mrs Bramley brought home these adorable baby animals. They knew the future was no longer going to be peaceful, but the cat and the dog were going to try to and help take care of the kittens and puppies that already were making themselves at home.

The End

ALL THE OTHER EXCELLENT STORIES…

STORIES FROM WRITERS IN THE 3-7 YEARS OLD AGE GROUP

Florence Mellon, 3 years old

Once upon a time there was a Cat and a Dog.

The Dog was called Ralph.

The Cat was called Selwin.

They were best friends and they went to the park together.

At the park they saw a Unicorn on the slide and a big Tiger on the swings.

The Tiger Roared at Ralph and made him jump. Selwin played with the tiger and said hello.

Ralph went to play with the Unicorn and they all played together.

THE END

Mason Oliver Briggs, 3 years old

Once upon a time there was a cat and a dog.

The cat ate a gingerbread man and the dog ate some too.

Then they got on a green train.

The train went to Mason's house.

The dog and cat went inside Mason's house and they saw a bug!

It was a buzzy bee.

The dog said, "Thank you," because the bee was busy doing jobs outside.

The dog and cat went to sleep in a cat and dog bed.

The End.

Emily Hartley, 4 years old

Once upon a time there was a cat and a dog. The cat was all alone with no neighbours and then no friends come behind her and then a dog found her and then they were friends. And then there was an Alicorn and then no pegusi come. And then there were sweeties come, flower sweeties and they were yucky because they had got all of the honey.

They planted the flower sweeties and then they didn't do it all alone. And then a bad dragon come and then he started to do fire on the dog's tail and then the cat just saved the dog. And then there was sweetie floor and sweetie road and gingerbread houses and gingerbread people all in the country and gingerbread animals in the zoo.

The End

Myles-Gerard Jenkins, 4 years old

Once upon a time there was a cat and a dog.

The cat was called Ocean and the dog was called Jenkino.

They were very good friends and go on holiday to Spain together.

They travelled by car and train.

They played I Spy and Uncle Ged met them in Spain.

He travelled by Aeroplane.

The cat and the dog took their human mummy Kelly and their human brothers Myles and Teddy with them.

They both fed the cat and the dog.

Myles and Teddy fed Ocean and Mummy fed Jenkino.

Oliver and Summer, Myles and Teddy's cousins both had swimming pools.

They let the cat and the dog swim in them.

Rafe Newton, 5 years old

Once there was a cat and a dog.

They were playing in the ball pit.

They slided down the slide.

Next they went home and had a big hug.

They had a rest watching T.V.

The end.

Anabel Berry

Once upon a time there was a cat and a dog. The cat was desperate for food. His stomach was empty and felt a rumble every two seconds.

The dog wasn't hungry at all. He was healthy, fit, strong and fearless. Every time the cat's belly juddered, he glanced at the dog. Usually he took a little look at his meaty legs.

Suddenly, the cat leaped and bit the dog. All the dog did was weep. The cat fell and the dog ran off.

The end.

Sienna Frow, 5 years old

Once up on a time there was a cat and a dog making a sandcastle together. The cat called Goldy shouted to her friend Paddy the spotty dog that she was going for a paddle in the sea.

Goldy tripped over a rock and fell into the sea. She asked Paddy for help. Paddy had his superhero costume on so he flew to rescue Goldy from the sea.

He carries Goldy to the vets to look at her leg that was bleeding and she had banged her face too. The vet bandages the legs to stop it bleeding and put a special cream on her face. The special cream made Goldy better and turned her into a princess cat with a pretty dress covered with sparkly gems.

Paddy put on his shiny collar. They got married and lived happily ever after.

The End.

Joseph Nelson, 5 years old

Once upon a time there was a cat and a dog. They played with a ball together. A bird meeted them and said hello.

They met a frog at the pond and played hide and seek. A bat came and flyed around to make the cat and dog laugh.

They went to play football outside in the mud and got dirty and dogs love washes. The cat ran away. Frog came after they had a wash and they had a jumping competition and all the frogs came.

The cat comed back for fish and eat it all and licked her lips. The dog ate Spam. And then they curled up and went to sleep.

Cora Murray, 5 years old

Once upon a time there was a cat and a dog and their names were Sarah and Florence.

They were very good friends until Sarah found Florence sleeping in her bed.

Florence was very cross because Sarah got all the best sleeping places.

Their owner was very sad because her pets seemed so unhappy.

She decided to buy them a giant bed that they could both share.

Sarah and Florence never argued again.

The End

Sienna Duke, 5 years old

Once up on a time there was a dog called Lexi Lou. She was a little Shih tzu. She loved to play and eat treats all day long. One day when she was out and about a pussycat came up to her and said, "Hey, what are you doing in my neighbourhood? You are not allowed. Go away back to where you belong and not on my patch. I'm the king of these streets," but Lexi Lou wouldn't have it. She turned around on the pussy cat and said, "You're mean. You are just a bully and this neighbourhood is for EVERYONE to share. SHARING IS CARING." This is the motto of Lexi Lou. She loved everyone and everything. The cat was shocked and walked away but had learned a lesson that not everyone was scared of her. Later the community that had all been scared of going out because of the mean pussycat has heard of Lexi Lou's bravery and they wasn't frightened no more. They arranged a street party to celebrate everyone's freedom. While everyone was enjoying the party Lexi Lou couldn't help but think about the poor pussy cat and went to find her. When Lexi Lou found the pussy cat she was so sad and said, "Sorry, I really just want to be friends," so Lexi Lou asked, "Why have you been mean then? We will be your friend. Come back to the party with me," so the mean pussycat said, "O.k., thank you for your forgiveness. My name is Ivy," and they became best friends.

So the moral of the story is: don't let people bully you. Always stand up for yourself and everything will be ok.

The end

Florence Baker, 6 years old

Once upon a time there was a cat and a dog. The cat was called Amos and the dog was called Beau. They met at the park every day. They were best friends. One night they were looking at the big, white moon. They saw a pattern in it. "There's a rabbit in the moon!" Beau shouted. Amos said, "It's just a pattern."

So they jumped into their giant, black and red shiny rumbling fire -shooting rocket and they set off to go to space! When they got to the moon they knocked on the floor. Then in a boom shaka laka a big rabbit appears. The rabbit said "Do you want a picnic Amos and Beau?" "Yes but one thing, how do you know our names?" they asked the big furry soft rabbit. "I know everyone's names," he said to them. "Have you got everything for the picnic?" Beau asked. The rabbit said yes.

So they got on with the picnic. The rabbit said, "Close your eyes and imagine what you would like to eat." Beau said he wanted to eat ice cream. Amos said he wanted cat ice cream. In a puff of smoke the food came to them. After they had their food they said goodbye and they went back home. When they got back home they waved at the rabbit and this time he waved back.

Guy Gozzard, 6 years old

(A slight spin on Once upon a time there was a cat and a dog…)

Once upon a time a king was relaxing on his hammock.

All of a sudden a book appeared.

He opened it.

A man appeared with a gun. He said, "Put your hands up!"

The king climbs a tree. He shouts, "Get away!"

The gangster shoot him.

The gangster takes off his clothes and turns into a spy.

He dragged him to his boss. His boss said, "Who's that?"

"It's the person you wanted."

"No, it's not! I wanted the king up the road!"

The End.

Hollie Preston, 6 years old

Once upon a time there lived a dog. The dog she is called Lilly. Lilly is very young. She is 3. She is 3 like my brother. My brother is called Harry. Lilly has a mum. Her mum is called Ivy. Ivy is 39. Ivy was sick so me and my brother rushed to the vets. Ivy was really sick like my brother except my brother is not a dog he's a human. Ivy is a dog not a human.

The vet said, "You can go home now." We said, "Thank you very much." We went home and it was a bit funny because then Lilly got sick because she caught it. We went to vets again. This time the vet said, "Keep an eye on Lilly. She'll get better soon," and we went home. My brother was on candy crush. He is on level 59. I was watching FROZEN 2.

Alfie Price, 6 years old

Once upon a time there was a cat and a dog who were best friends. They had a friend called Humphrey who wasn't very kind. Humphrey tried to eat cat and dog's food, "We need to share," said cat and dog. But Humphrey didn't like to share. He hid cat and dog's toys. "We need to share," said cat and dog. But Humphrey didn't like to share.

One day Humphrey lost his favourite toy bus. He was so sad. Cat and dog said, "We will help you look for your bus." But Humphrey just cried.

Cat and dog went searching for the bus. They looked under the table and under the chair but it wasn't there. "Let's look outside." Cat found the bus on the slide. They took the bus back to Humphrey who was so grateful, he gave cat and dog a big smile. "Thank you," he said.

Cat, dog and Humphrey became best friends. They shared all their food and all of their toys and was very kind to each other which made them very happy. They all lived happily ever after.

The End.

Ivy Hawes, 6 years old

The dog was called Coco and the cat was called Betty and they lived in a den down the street. They always loved seeing Mr Globe and his Family. They loved his shop because it was nice, lovely, pretty and beautiful. His real name is Mike. His wife is Stacey, his son is George and his daughter is Jessica.

They had a colourful globe. Coco accidentally knocked over the glass globe. Clever Betty said, "I will fix it." So she fixed it. They all worked as a team to tidy the shop. In the morning they all went on a big forest adventure.

They built a wigwam. They camped and slept all night there. They did loads of activities. They were having fun. They found some leaves to take back to decorate the wigwam. The cat was very dirty so Betty had a bath.

All of them was excited to sleep in the wigwam. So they went to bed. In the morning they packed to go home. But they left the wigwam behind. They went home before the cat and dog went home in their den. They stayed at Mr Globe's shop. Then they went home. Coco chewed on his bone. They both had a nap. When they woke up they had a dance and they bought loads of stuff from Mr Globe's shop.

THE END

Madison Wrigglesworth, 6 years old

Once upon a time there was a cat and a dog. Molly and Ben got lost on Saturday in the forest and their home was at Mosberry Road.

They were scared because the people was mean to them.

Their parents was even meaner because they needed a bath. Some nice people found Molly and Ben and took them to the village.

On Sunday they went to look for their parents but a really bad storm was coming and it was good but they were sad because their parents were dead.

They lived happily ever after with their new family.

Oliver Booth, 6 years old

One hot day the owners went shopping and left the dog at home. Luna the dog was crying and howling when all of a sudden in jumped a white cat and sat next to the open window. "Miiaaoow!" shouted the cat.

Luna barked and chased the cat all over the house. The cat was a happy and friendly cat and turned around and gave Luna a lick on the nose.

The cat and the dog became friends. They played ball- and - string inside and had a lovely time together.

All of a sudden they heard the owners coming back. The cat quickly hid under the table and miaoowed!

The people looked under the table and saw the white cat. Luna gave her a humongous lick. "Shall we keep her?" said the mummy. "We will call her Snowflake!"

They lived happily ever after.

The end.

Abigail Booth, 6 years old

One hot day Sophie the dog was chasing her tail and playing in the garden.

Suddenly an orange stripey cat jumped over the fence and Sophie noticed it was her friend, Emily. Every day Emily came to play with her friend Sophie and played hide and seek around the garden. They played chase in the house, they shared milk together and a nice snack together.

All of a sudden they heard the owners coming back home.

When the owners opened the door and then they saw Emily the cat and they said, "Oh what a pretty cat, maybe we should keep it."

Sophie and Emily were really happy to live together and they lived happily ever after.

The end.

Brooke Laird Smith, 6 years old

Once upon a time there were a cat and a dog.

They lived together in animal the sanctuary.

They were happy together but wanted a loving home.

One day a family came to visit the sanctuary and fell in love with the cat and the dog and took them home to live happily every after.

The End

Ellie Mae Andrews, 6 years old

Once upon a time there was a cat and a dog who were playing together at the park. They were playing hide and seek and the playful cat was trying to find the cheeky dog.

She was searching all around the playground until she heard a really loud bark coming from behind the bushes and the bush was moving!

The cat was feeling giddy because she thought it might be dog! Cat was right as dog appeared from behind the wobbling bush.

Dog and cat bursted out laughing and they rolled onto the floor.

Cat and dog went home but they stopped by at the ice-cream shop to pick up some ice-cream as a Happy Way to end the exciting sunny day.

Heidi Coleman, 6 years old

The Lost Kitten

One day a cat was hiding under a bed, and it was a kitten but it didn't have a name. He was under the bed because he was scared, so he stayed under.

Zoe was so excited to get to her house after the road work had been done. She was finally going back home. When she got home she heard a miaow.

It was a kitten! It was a grey tabby kitten and a very small one. "How did you get here!" All the kitten had to say was "miaow". Zoe just laughed and said, "You're so funny!" She kept it a secret.

Dad shouted, "Zoe, lunch is ready; come down now." So Zoe hid the kitten under the bed and went down to have her lunch. While she was having her lunch Dad went into Zoe's bedroom and found the kitten and was shocked. Zoe had thought of a name which was Miaow. Then Zoe said, "I found him under the bed."

"Then why didn't you tell me?" said Dad. Zoe said, "Sorry." Then they took him to the vets. The vet said, "Try to find his owner or you can keep him." But they couldn't find his owner so they had to keep him and they called him Miaow.

Jemima Roberts, 7 years old

One day a puppy called Sparky went to his best friend in the pet sanctuary. Her name was Misty and they loved adventures.

They were playing with some old tennis balls when they noticed the window was open. They looked at each other mischievously. They were going to escape. When nobody was looking, they silently tiptoed through the gap where the window should have been. They were in awe to see how huge the outside world was.

In a fur, paw, claw game (the pets' secret version of the popular game, rock, paper, scissors) it was decided that they should turn left. They made their way through crowds of stressed adults and screaming children as they took a shortcut through the busy supermarket. Angry shop owners chased after them in annoyance, but they managed to flee before they could be caught. They didn't stop running until they could no longer hear the heavy footsteps of the Tesco manager. When it was obvious that they were no longer being pursued, they took a break for the night under a park bench.

They awoke to loud cheers coming from the mouths of the smallest of people. Toddlers ran in every direction – clamouring for first go on the slide. They knew they must make an exit when a grubby child's hand grabbed towards their faces.

Dashing away through endless streets, they saw their home at last. This adventure had been fun, but they couldn't wait for a cosy night in with their friends.

Callum Wrigglesworth, 7 years old

Trip to the Beach

Once upon a time there was a cat and a dog. They were called Jack and Billy.

They were best friends.

One day, Jack and Billy went to the beach and they were playing with a beach ball and a bucket and spade.

Jack said he wanted to go swimming but the water was too cold.

Billy wanted to go treasure- hunting instead. All we found is an old shopping cart and an old leather boot.

Billy and Jack decided to go and have a donut before they set off home to bed. They lived happily ever after.

Charlotte Wright-Hobson, 7 years old

Tiger's and Pepsi's Adventure.

Once upon a time, there was a cat called Tiger and a dog called Pepsi.

Pepsi was a naughty dog but Tiger was nice.

But one day, the gate was opened so Pepsi and Tiger ran out to explore.

Pepsi found bones and Tiger found a tree so Tiger climbed up it and got stuck and Pepsi found a phone and called a fire truck. The fire truck rescued the cat so then they kept on playing but they were getting hungry so they found stuff to eat.

After they ate their food, they found a river and a boat.

So they went on the boat but it started to rain so they tried to go home but they couldn't but then they found a way home and they was at home and they said, "I never want to leave again."

Bella Auty, 7 years old

Once upon a time there was a cat and a dog. The cat's name was Baby and the dog's name was Rosie.

One day Rosie was on a walk in the park and saw Baby peeking out of a window. They barked and meowed at each other and their eyes met. From then on Rosie and Baby sneaked out to meet each other. The ginger cat purred as they fell in love.

Their friendly owners met up and they had a wonderful time together. They soon discovered Baby and Rosie were in love and Rosie was going to have a baby.

The baby was born, strangely looking a bit like a puppy but a bit like a kitten too! Sometimes she barked, sometimes she meowed. The owners stared softly at the new baby as she wagged her tail like a pup and ran off quickly to a lake and caught a fish with its sharp claws.

The new baby was called Docala and was loved sweetly by everyone in town, especially her parents Rosie the dog and Baby the cat. They all lived happily ever after.

The End.

Fenn Hardwick, 7 years old

Once upon a time, there was a cat and a dog called Freddy and Harry. Freddy the cat was black and white and Harry was big and brown. Freddy and Harry was playing catch in the garden.

Freddy accidentally put his claw in the ball ... POP! ... it went. Harry said, "Don't worry, let's go on a bike ride."

Harry jumped on the bike while Freddy checked the tire ... POP! ... it went.

Harry said, "Don't worry, we can play tag instead."

Freddy said "O.k!" Freddy accidentally scratched Harry's paw. "OUCH! he said.

"Don't worry, I know what we can play that you won't damage."

Harry brought out some big red gloves. "We can have a boxing match!"

Freddy was amazed and they played all day.

THE END

Maria Adele Scully, 7 years old

"Once upon a time there was a cat and a dog. A cat and a dog were walking around for ages looking for villains. "That is a dinosaur bone," said super dog! Oh well! That minute they heard a ROAR! "I'm scared," said super cat. "It is not real."

"Ok," said super cat. They turned around and saw a dinosaur. "RUN," cried super dog. They ran as fast as they can and they saw a dragon in the sky and went down low to hide and then they saw a home. They went inside.

They stayed in the home and later the dinosaur came in and super dog said, "What are you doing here?" The dinosaur replied, "This is my house so get out!" They ran and ran. They saw another home and went inside and later that day the dragon came inside. "This is my house, get out." They ran.

They ran to a field and on the way they found 2 swords. Super dog and super cat got one each and went to kill the dinosaur and the dragon. Super dog went to the dinosaur and killed him by swinging his sword. Super cat went to the dragon and killed him with a sword. Super dog and super cat had won.

They were walking around after. "Who will we beat tomorrow?" said super dog. " I don't know," said super cat, "but I am not scared anymore."

George Brown, 7 years old

The Rock Adventuremals

Once upon a time there was a cat and a dog who were lonely at Thornberry Animal Sanctuary and they loved all kinds of music.

One day they saw an advert about a music competition and the prize was lots of money, so they decided to make a band with their friends. If you are wondering who their friends are then read this…. their best friends were called Tipsy Turtle and Bertie Bear. The cat is called Cara and Daniel is the Dog. Now if you're clever you might want to know when the practice starts; well it starts in a week - so before you read on wait for a minute then it will feel like a week has passed….Now back to the story.

They decide to practise in Bertie's garage. Daniel plays guitar, Cara is lead singer, Bertie plays the drums and Tipsy plays the Trumpet. "We sound horrible," Tipsy angrily shouted. It took a lot of practice, but they were finally ready for the competition. But then out of nowhere – the devil took their invite, "Wa ha ha!!! Now WE can dress up as you, do the concert and WIN!" The devil vanished into a puff of air.

Meanwhile, the band snook into the lair using the HELL (High-Electronic-Life-Losers) Machine … BANG! All the devils saw them fall. Bertie said, "RUN!" and the devils chased them. "We want our tickets back," Bertie bravely said as he snatched them off him and ran back home.

The band did the concert and they won! They used the money they won to give all the lonely animals at Thornberry a home, including themselves. So, they really did live happily ever after.

THE END

Mason Bennett, 7 years old

Once upon a time there were a cat and a dog that loved to play together. The dog was called Alfie and the cat was called Snowflake; they followed each other everywhere. One day Snowflake went missing and Alfie felt lost without his best friend. Alfie's owners didn't understand why Alfie was not eating his food and looking so sad. They tried playing catch with Alfie but he would just watch the ball fly past his head.

One morning when Alfie's owners opened the door Alfie rushed out of the house and ran straight up the road. This was not like Alfie at all. No matter how many times the owners shouted at him to come back he just carried on running. Alfie had gone hunting for Snowflake and was not giving up until he had found her safe and sound. Alfie searched the local fields, the park and every place that they would go together but he just had no luck finding her. Alfie became more sad and worried. He really was puzzled; this was just not like Snowflake. It was getting late so Alfie decided he best go home before his owners got too worried.

On the way home Alfie heard some people talking. He heard them say that they had taken a lost cat to the animal sanctuary so that it could be cared for and hopefully find a loving new home. He just knew that they were talking about Snowflake. Alfie knew he had to go search for the animal sanctuary. He began walking to find it. It felt like he had been walking forever. Just then Alfie saw a sign that said Thornberry Animal Sanctuary so he took himself inside.

When he got in there there was lots of different dogs and cats. He walked past them all and right at the very end was Snowflake. Alfie quickly let her out and led her back home. When they got home, the owners was so pleased to see them and they was pleased to see their owners too. They ate all their dinners up and went out in the garden to play ball. They were happy once again and from this day on they never left each other's sides again.

Rose Gilbert-Clark, 7 years old
Fluffy and Frank.

Once upon a time there was a cat called Fluffy and a dog called Frank, who lived in an old creaky house with a little old woman. Frank was playing with his favourite toy when Fluffy swiped his bone and dashed off. Frank felt furious, so he chased after her. Fluffy ran into an abandoned forest next to their house. She climbed a tall narrow tree so Frank couldn't reach her. But suddenly there was a SNAP! The branch the she was standing on, split and was hanging on by a tiny thread! Fluffy meowed for help MEOW, MEOW. It was no use as the old woman wouldn't be able to hear her.

Then from out of nowhere a witch came zooming in on a broomstick and grabbed Fluffy just as she slipped off and was falling to the ground. She sat Fluffy on the broomd, who was clinging on for her life when she spotted Frank on the ground. They both looked at each other wondering what had just happened. Who was this witch?

Frank followed them as the witch landed outside their house and took off her hat.It was the little old woman. Was the little old woman really a witch? Fluffy and Frank thought she was a little bit strange but not a witch. What would she do with them now they have found out that she is actually a witch?

Ruby Hemingway, 7 years old

Once upon a time there was a cat and a dog. The dog was 3 and the cat was 4.

One day some people walked inside the pet shop. It was a little girl, called Ruby, with her mum and her dad. They were looking for a pet. The animals really wanted an owner but the family walked straight past. Then as soon as they came back they had no pet in their hands. They looked at the dog and the cat and picked them both up. Ruby said, "I think these pets are right for me."

As soon as she purchased the dog and the cat they went to a shop to buy them some toys. It said, "No animals allowed inside" so they tied them both up on the lamp-post. They both felt sad as they went into the shop without them. They both broke the lead and ran off because they didn't feel loved enough. They ran into a library but it was crowded. However they managed to squeeze through and someone picked them up and took them to the police.

At the same time the new owners were looking all over, the dogs were really confused as to their big adventure that day. As soon as the family realised they had lost their pets they went to the police and found their dog and cat. They were so happy.

STORIES FROM WRITERS IN THE 8-10 YEARS OLD AGE GROUP

Grace Morris, 8 years old

Once upon a time there was a cat and a dog. The cat was called Rupert. His favourite thing was laying in the sun and eating lots of sardines. He would eat them for breakfast, lunch, dinner and lots of sardine snacks in between.

He never exercised and was very lazy! Each day he just got bigger and BIGGER.

Every morning he went through the cat flap to be in the sunshine and every day it was getting more and more tricky to squeeze through. Ollie the dog could fit through with ease. He was a Border Terrier and loved chasing balls in the garden. He wasn't lazy like Rupert.

One day Rupert woke up and waddled over to the cat flap. He put his head through and his front paws but then.... oh no! He got stuck! His tummy was too big. He shouted Ollie for help. Ollie tried to push him out but it only made things worse. He put butter on Rupert but it just matted his fur. None of their plans worked. They needed extra help.

Ollie called for Jasper and Stan, the neighbour's dogs. Jasper, the Patterdale, loved playing with tug toys so he would be perfect for helping Ollie pull Rupert at the front. Stan was a strong German Shepherd. Pushing Rupert from behind should be a piece of cake. "In position," Ollie shouted. "1...2...3" And Rupert shot in the air. "Phew" they heard him sigh."Thanks guys! Perhaps it's time for me to go on a diet...but not before one more tin of sardines.

Fatima Rehman, 8 years old

Once upon a time, a lonely cat was stuck in the middle of nowhere. She tried to find her way out but she was too scared. She was scared of the dark. There were various coloured keys she had to find to escape. But she also had to look out for the killer Bakon.

First she found the blue key. The blue key went to the back of the haunted forest. It was really hard because the haunted forest was actually a haunted maze. After that, she found the purple key. That key went to the house to get the bridge. Then she found the books. When she put all of them in she found the key to escape.

But Bakon the killer cat was guarding the escape door. So she tried to outsmart him but when she tried to do it Bakon almost killed her but she escaped. But she ended up in big trouble because she was trapped again. But this time the only thing to do was to find the key. But it was hard because the key was hidden so well.

Then she cried, "Dang it, I can't escape yet." She tried to climb the door but there was nothing she could do about it. Then she thought, "If I was Bakon, where would I hide the key? I got it, in the kitchen." She found the key and she escaped.

Harriet Hopkins, 8 years old

Once upon a time there was a cat called Whiskers and a dog called Ruffles. Whiskers lived in an old dusty house and Ruffles lived in a smelly dump. They had one thing in common, they were abandoned.

One rainy Sunday afternoon, Whiskers went for a walk in a field and Ruffles went to the same field. Whiskers was running around the field to catch a little mouse but before she could catch it Ruffles caught the mouse. Whiskers was mad and said, '' That's my tea you beast.'' Ruffles looked down at the mouse and said, ''Sorry'' and gave it her back.

''You're a dog; you don't catch mice. You should chase me,'' said Whiskers looking confused at Ruffles. '' I don't like chasing cats,'' said Ruffles. Then Ruffles' tummy made a loud noise, so Whiskers shared the mouse with Ruffles.

''Thank you,'' said Ruffles. As Ruffles turned to walk home Whiskers shouted ''STOP, STOP!''

''Can I come live with you? I don't like my dusty house on my own.'' Ruffles was shocked and smiled, ''Yes, come with me.I am Ruffles.''

''I am Whiskers,'' Whiskers replied quickly.

It was still raining on that damp and cold Sunday afternoon. When they both arrived back to the smelly dump there was people there. It was people from Thornberry Animal Sanctuary. They picked up Whiskers and Ruffles and took them to the warm and clean sanctuary.

A week later a lady came and took Whiskers and Ruffles to their forever home.

Freddie Pevitt, 8 years old

Once upon a time there was a cat called Midnight and a greyhound dog called Jack. They were moving home on a plane. They were as excited as children going to the beach. Frolicking around with excitement, they jumped and twirled.

Suddenly the cage they shared in the hold department popped open. CRASH! Fire burst the door open. They began slipping and sliding from side to side until they started floating for a moment in the air. BANG! The plane had crashed into a deserted beach. They worked together to push open the emergency door.

They emerged from the wreck, searching for their owners…but couldn't see them. They gazed ahead and was greeted with a mysterious forest. Mist was swirling around them as they tiptoed through the forest. Flickers of glow worms illuminated a magical path to a lake. Moonlight shone on the silver grass like thousands of tiny mirrors. Beyond the fog was a beautiful landscape. Magical and mythical creatures roamed the land.

As they stood there, open- mouthed, a mysterious creature stumbled up to them. "You're new!" he said playfully. "Do you need somewhere to stay?" The two shocked animals nodded their head in unison.

The rest of the evening was spent feasting on delicious berries, meeting the locals and exploring their new home. Purple sprouting lava volcanoes and crystallized caverns was just the beginning of their adventure. Even though the mystery of their beloved owners was weighing on their heart…they knew this was where they belong.

Ruqayya Hussain, 8 years old

The lost cat in New York

Once upon a time there was a cat and a dog. They lived in New York City. The cat was called Roxy and the dog was called Sam. Sam didn't have an owner but Roxy's owner was called Ruqayya. Sam was a lonely little dog.

Ruqayya and Roxy went ice- skating but Roxy got lost in the crowd. But the next day Ruqayya put out some posters and Sam saw the poster and thought......Uhmm, I have seen this cat before. Roxy was worried when she got lost and she went to the biggest Christmas tree in the world. Sam was all alone on Christmas so he went near the Christmas tree and found Roxy. Sam went up to her and said, "Are you lost?" "Yes I am,'' replied Roxy. "I can help you'' replied Sam.

They went into the woods until they saw a mysterious boy. He was shouting ROXY! When she got closer she knew that the little boy was her owner's brother called Shoaib. Roxy asked Shoaib, "Can you take us to Ruqayya please?"

"Yes follow me," replied Shoaib. Ruqayya was crying but she saw Roxy and Roxy saw her. They ran towards each other and hugged. Ruqayya thanked Sam for finding Roxy and she had a surprise for him.

When they got home Ruqayya threw a party and people weren't being mean and horrible to Sam. They all became best friends and Sam had an owner which was Ruqayya's brother, Shoaib! They all lived happily ever after.

Chloe Dudill, 8 years old

On the 17th of March 2020 a dog sat outside his house on the steps. "What a wonderful day," said the little dog to himself. As it was quiet he heard the cat next door speaking to herself. She said, "What a bright sunny day to sit in the sun and sunbathe.'' That night the cat went on an adventure to search for a mouse and the dog went out for a run. Suddenly, they didn't know where they were which means they were…

LOST! What were they going to do? They didn't know where to sleep; the only place they could see was under an old oak tree. The next morning, the cat heard something. It sounded like the dog next door so she woke up and followed the sound.

She found the dog next door panicking and upset. She introduced herself to the dog. She said, "Hello, my name is Flower. What is your name?" The dog said, "My name is Billy. I got lost last night and I have never been lost in my entire life. I am so scared." Flower knew that Billy was panicking. What could she do?

"Do you want to build a treehouse to live in; we can look after each other and have lots of adventures?" Flower said. Billy replied, "Yes I would like that." From that day they became the best of friends.

Kitt Fox, 8 years old

Hi, I'm that cat. My name is Tiddles and my friend the dog is called Fred.

One day Tiddles and Fred had a big fight over some food and fell out so Tiddles pulled a trick on Fred. She filled his bowl with mud.

When he ate it, he knew it was Tiddles who did it so her got her back.

Fred decided to throw a ball of yarn outside and locked Tiddles outside but they apologised and became friends again and lived happily ever after.

The End

Daniel Drury, 8 years old

Cake town

Once upon a time there was a cat and a dog and they found a town and it was made out of cake. They found a hotel and the pool was melted chocolate! "URGH, chocolate!" they said.

"Oh, my name is Sid, the cat and this is my friend Steve, the dog. We hate chocolate as you heard". "I feel a bit sick!" they said."Where is the toilet?" they said. Suddenly a cake monster spotted Sid the cat "SID!", shouted Steve."Oh no!" said Sid. "What is that?" said Steve as something whizzed past leaving floating marshmallows behind!! "Supermarshmallow to the rescue!"she said. "OMG!" they said, "I love your movies back at home!!"

"Do you? No time to talk!" she said. "I just talked to Supermarshmallowgirl in person!!!" said Sid excitedly. "Help!" said marshmallow girl.

"Quickly, she needs our help" said Steve. BANG, SMACK, BASH "Yes, it has given up, we win once again!".

They jump in the pool. "Oh no, I forgot what the pool is made of - chocolate sauce, yum!" said marshmallowgirl happily. "I could do this all day."

"I loved that day," they said and they lived happily ever after.

The End.

Madelaine Jones, 8 years old

ONCE UPON A TIME THERE WAS A CAT AND A DOG...who lived in a pet sanctuary and were treated very kindly. Eventually, the furry kitten and the cute dog got taken to a new house together with another dog, who was a Bulldog. The family took care of their pets very well, especially the little girl, who was polite and kind.

The dogs and the kitten always wondered what it would be like to be wild. They were served a delicious breakfast and were ready for an adventure in the park. The weird thing about this family is they put a dog lead on the kitten!

The pets got free and ran off with the little girl. They ran as fast as the wind, although the Bulldog was older and a little slower. Soon they were in the city and had lost their owners, so the little girl cried. However, her worried parents soon came into sight.

The next day the pets snuck out to thc park again and played games. The bulldog was hungry and ate something bad out of the rubbish bin. Two days later the Bulldog still looked ill, so the family took him to the vet, who said he wasn't going to live much longer as he had been poisoned. Then the bulldog was gone. The kitten and the dog lived a happy life, but missed their good friend, the Bulldog.

Riley Sykes, 8 years old

There was once a cat called Fuzzy McFuzz and a dog called Fluffer. They were best friends and they didn't have owners or homes. They also lived on the cold, dark and crowded street. The other bad thing is, IT WAS WORLD WAR 2! Also, they lived near the battle ground!

One day, the army found Fluffer and took him away. That was the last time Fuzzy McFuzz saw Fluffer. The next day Fuzzy McFuzz went to find Fluffer. She looked all over town and he was nowhere. Then she thought he could have been taken to the battleground, the only forbidden place in town.

So Fuzzy McFuzz went to the battleground and found Fluffer but the army was trying to train him to be an army dog. He looked bigger and buffer than ever before. When the army went to fight, Fuzzy McFuzz tried to talk to Fluffer. "It's me, Fuzzy McFuzz," said Fuzzy McFuzz. Fluffer made a surprised face but still believed her and came with her but they got caught but Fuzzy McFuzz jumped on his head! They ran so fast just to get to the start of the city but their part of it was at the other side!

Fuzzy McFuzz and Fluffer jumped on big buildings and bounced on colourful umbrellas until finally they got to the other side. But the other problem was they needed to get to their alleyway. They jumped on the taxi to get there.

Parker Bradley, 8 years old

Once upon a time there was a cat and a dog,

They lived happily together with Janice and Bob,

Doing everything together as best friends do,

Over the years the closer they grew.

But…

At night where did the clever cat go?

Dog decided he wanted to know.

So, at bedtime…

Knowing the kitchen window wasn't quite shut,

Just wide enough for a dog's furry butt…

Cat went out first and waited outside,

Next came dog with a THUD!

He cried.

He didn't land perfectly on all fours,

He banged his head and hurt his paws.

But it did look beautiful out under the stars,

So peaceful and calm without any cars.

Let's go …

They explored the alleyway looking for rats,

But dogs aren't good at sneaking like cats,

Cat found a delicious midnight snack,

A smelly fish bone that made the dog yack!

Try this…

Cat jumped on the wall to get a good view,

But this wasn't something dog could do.

Cat dug up the flower bed that looked like fun,

He made a small hole and sat on his bum,

What was Dog's friend about to do?

Dog couldn't believe it, he was doing a ***

Yuck!!!

That's it thought dog, enough was enough,

There's no poo bags or humans to come pick that up!

So off home he ran (tripping over a hedgehog and a tin can)

Into the window and onto his bed,

I'll stay in at night now the sleepy dog said.

Goodnight Dog.

Poppy Frow, 8 years old

Once upon a time there was a dog and a cat, who were the best of friends. The cat was Ginger and had eyes as large as saucers. Her name was Willow and she had a pink nose and sharp claws. The dog was a Pug and was brown. Also he had hazel eyes that were extremely giant and round and he had a blue collar with a really shimmery diamond on it.

One day, Willow and Ted were playing together in the garden when Willow accidentally scratched Ted and he was in lots of pain. He was bleeding on his paw and on his leg at the back. Willow went to tell her owner and she gasped when she heard about it. She picks up Ted and Willow follows behind and they clamber into the car to the vets.

The vets needed to do an x-ray to see if there was any damage to bones. To their surprise the scratches went to the bones so they gave Ted an anaesthetic to send him to sleep for the big operation. The vets get prepared too. Twenty minutes later the operation is finally finished.

Willow felt very guilty for Ted but just as Willow was putting her head down to cry the vets said that there is no scratches anymore and everyone was joyful again. Ted and Willow said sorry to each other.

When they arrived back home Ted and Willow ran to the sofa and settled down together, friends again.

Patrick Prescott, 8 years old

ROLO AND SHADOW

Once upon a time, there was a cat and a dog. The cat was called Rolo and the dog was called Shadow. Rolo and Shadow were great friends. The breed that Shadow is, is a German Shepherd and he is brown and black. When, Shadow goes on his walk, Rolo always follows. Anywhere Shadow goes Rolo follows because they are both best friends. It is very funny because Shadow is tall and Rolo is small.

At bedtime they both sleep together and cuddle together. One day Shadow went on his walk and obviously Rolo followed but something really funny happened. Rolo jumped on Shadow's back and played together. When they got back to the house Rolo and Shadow went in the garden together and played with each other. They tried to play lots of sports like football or be an athlete and run and they did so much stuff together.

The next day Shadow went on his walk with his owner and Rolo and they were on their way home and the owner dropped his wallet and that wasn't good because it had all his money in and his credit cards but he had not noticed but he still has hope because Shadow is still going to walk past it but he didn't see it so there was no hope.

When they got home Shadow realised so he ran back and found it on the floor. He brought it back with Rolo and got to sleep with the owner.

Abeera Kazmi, 8 years old

Once upon a time, there was a cat and a dog. The cat's name was Winnie and the dog was called Wonder. Winnie loved to move from one spot to another and rest for 5 minutes at each corner. But Wonder was tons more alive and energetic; she always used to wear her owner Lilly's clothing and walked on the runway!

One sunny day 7:00, Lilly went to work as the fake sleeping pets slept on their scratch castle or dog tent. As soon as Lilly shut the door, Wonder bounced off the bed and ran off to the forest. Wonder's family lived there but she refused and turned back; guess who was there, WINNIE. She had the meanest look ever on her face; she was crossing her arms as well. Wonder and Winnie were thinking the exact same thing.

"Thinking what I'm thinking?" asked Winnie. "I don't know." said Wonder. "Ruined the whole scene right? Anyways, let's go on a trip!"

This is like the only time Winnie agreed to go. On their way, they felt scared.

"Umm let's go home," moaned Wonder. Winnie nudged Wonder. "See that huge tree there, that's where the cat hut is," whispered Winnie. "Let's go in!"said Wonder, the instagram famous poodle. "Are you out of your mind! The rumour has it that any dog that goes in will be sucked into it."

That's when Lilly came back. Her jaw fell to the ground as her skin became pale white! She was still cross until the pets came home. She was really furious!

They grew older and wiser after days.

Harry Barber, 8 years old

Once upon a time there was a cat and dog called Barney and Ozzy. They are superheroes but there are two evil pigs called Rodney Trotter and Pinky Pig. The pigs loved stealing things from Thornberry Rescue Centre. They have tried to steal the animals, medical supplies and drinks, but Barney and Ozzy stopped them. This time they took it too far; they had stolen the food and Barney and Ozzy loved food!

Barney and Ozzy were furious with the pigs. Barney wanted to scratch them and Ozzy wanted to bite them. Barney the Cat jumped on Ozzy's back and Ozzy ran all the way to the evil Pigs' lair. When they arrived there were no evil pigs to be seen anywhere but there were other pigs guarding the entrance. They tried to deafen Barney and Ozzy with their loud honks, but then Barney jumped on to the roof, climbed up near the roof and managed to get past them. Ozzy wagged his tail so fast that it scattered the guard pigs for miles around.

Once inside they found the missing food. "Just two more enemies to defeat," woofed Ozzy. All of a sudden the two evil pigs Rodney Trotter and Pinky Pig arrived. They honked as loud as they could. Ozzy dog had very sensitive ears and this made him jump and run away from the noise. Barney jumped out of the way of the noise. Once Ozzy had recovered from the scare, he ran straight back and barged Pinky Pig right out of the way. Rodney Trotter was very angry and he pulled out a pig lump of mud and threw it at Ozzy. Luckily Barney had made a shield with his paws and bounced the mud straight back at the pig hitting him in the face and covering his eyes. Seeing an opportunity, Barney jumped on Rodney Trotter's back and pushed him in to the nearest pig sty.

Barney and Ozzy grabbed up all the food and took it back to Thornberry Rescue Centre. They were met with cheers of joy from all the other animals."Hurray, our food is back, Thank you for saving us, Ozzy and Barney. We would have been so hungry if those evil pigs would have kept all of our yummie food."

Everybody lived happily ever after and the evil pigs never bothered the heroes of Thornberry ever again.

Abigail Jones, 8 years old

ONCE UPON A TIME THERE WAS A CAT AND A DOG…who lived in a pet sanctuary and had never been owned, not because they weren't wanted, but because every time somebody took one home, they came running back to the comfort of the pet sanctuary. The funny thing is the dog and the cat don't know each other and are kept far apart.

One day, an old man with a crooked chin and a black eye brought both the cat and the dog home, but he looked quite suspicious. Later, the cat and the dog realised it would be hard to escape this particular house, so here is where the adventure begins….

The brave cat jumped high and managed to grab the keys to the front door and the clever dog opened the door out of the room, but what they didn't realise was the house was full of red- eyed wolves. Suddenly, a wolf jumped out of the next room and hissed through his sharp teeth. The cat told the dog she had a plan. The cat handed the dog the key and began to act like a cute kitten to distract the wolves. It was working! The dog quietly fitted the key into the lock. The cat sprinted through the hall and out the door where the dog was waiting for her and soon they were back at the sanctuary.

Now they are kept next to each other so they can talk about their adventure.

Olivia Maia Heafield, 8 years old

Once upon a time there was a cat and a dog, who met each other in an animal sanctuary and became the best of friends. One cold winter's night they told each other their scary stories about how they ended in the animal sanctuary. The cat called Piper and the dog called Rusty. Piper started her story first…

It was the middle of halloween with fighting people wearing scary masks everywhere. But I was too busy chasing a mouse. WHEN a green scary which stepped out in front of me. I was so scared I jumped in fright. I jumped in the closest bush. It was very prickly and I ended up covered in sharp spikes. When I finally plucked up the courage to come out, I could hardly walk when a nice lady found me and brought me here. What about you Rusty?

Well I woke up one morning in the middle of a field and I couldn't find my mummy. So I decided to go and find her. While I was walking through the thick green grass I wasn't looking where I was going and I fell in a pond. When I came to the other side I was soaking wet and covered in smelly pond weeds. I managed to shake most of it off and carried on walking though the field. Wind was blowing me really hard and it made me really cold. I couldn't stand one more moment in this cold air. I lay down next to a bush and I was woken by a nice man who brought me here.

Piper and Rusty were so grateful to be safe and warm at Thornberry Animal Sanctuary.

Evie Crowther-Sheriff, 8 years old

One beautiful, sunny, morning, the birds were happily singing a peaceful song.

There was a dog called Harry. Harry got up that morning, got dressed for work and had waffles for breakfast as waffles were his favourite.

Harry the dog then got ready for work, where he sells cars. Meanwhile a new worker had started that day called David. IT WAS A CAT ! Cats are so sly and cheeky, that's the reason why Harry dislikes cats, so Harry that day went home confused about his new workmate. Harry had left-overs from yesterday for his tea which was yummy. Harry then got ready for bed. He thought about what tomorrow would bring. Harry got up that morning, birds still singing and had his normal waffles for breakfast and off to work he went.

Harry had a shock when he got to work, DAVID HAD STOLEN HARRY'S JOB. I TOLD YOU CATS WERE SLY! Harry went home, had no tea and just went straight to bed. Harry was upset and frustrated about what the sly cat had done.

So the following morning Harry awoke from a restless sleep. He didn't have breakfast and didn't get dressed for work. Harry just got up and went to the park.

Harry sat on a bench feeling blue, sad, and alone. Harry sat there with his eyes shut listening to the birds sing. Before long Harry felt a tap on his tail. Harry didn't look up straight away but on the floor he could see a shadow. To Harry's amazement it was a shadow of a cat.

It was David, coming to give Harry his job back. Harry was so happy and over the moon. David explained he didn't want to steal Harry's job; he wanted to help and become his friend. So over time Harry and David became the best of friends and did everything together.

Freya Sykes, 8 years old

One upon a time there lived a cat and dog called Oreo and Bear. Oreo was a small black and white cat and lived with Niamh. Bear was a fluffy ginger dog and was Freya's best friend. As we all know, dogs are attracted to rainbows but in this world they were no rainbows so Bear felt sad.

Oreo loved to cheer dogs up and was not a cat who is afraid ofdogs. They love each over to bits and Oreo had a plan! Bear counted on Oreo and they could amazingly understand each other. He said," We can sneak into a magical land." To Freya and Niamh this just sounded like MEOW and WOOF!

Oreo woke up a sleepy Bear. It was action. They were off to find a rainbow. They went through a magical bush and BANG there was a rainbow! Bear was crying with happiness but "How do we get to the end?" said Bear.

Oreo and Bear wanted to bring back treasure to Niamh and Freya. Shall we go over it or under it? The fun way was over it. It was like a slide. They held paws and zoomed down the slide, landing in a pile of treasure. They tried to get all the treasure they could but then they thought, No, let's not do that at this hard time, let's leave some for everyone else. They headed back home, hoping that Niamh and Freya wouldn't notice and luckily they were both fast asleep.

Maisy Foster, 9 years old

There was once an old, wrinkly lady. Her name was Miss Blue. Miss Blue had two pets, Gertrude and Cooper.

Gertrude was a very lazy cat. She had a big belly, two shiny eyes and soft, golden fur. Gertrude loved getting all the attention but she hated it when it was Cooper's turn to watch TV.

Cooper was a very jolly dog. He had long, floppy ears, a red bow on his tail and dark, curly fur. Cooper loved going on walks and playing fetch. He didn't like mean cats like Gertrude.

One day Cooper wanted to watch his favourite programme, Dog Boy and Cat Girl. Cooper went into the living room and saw Gertrude watching Garfield. Cooper went up to Gertrude and pushed her off the chair but Gertrude was strong and she climbed back on the chair.

Suddenly Miss Blue walked in and said, "Oh you cheeky animals, Bob is coming soon so be good." She then walked out the room with a grin on her face.

Gertrude and Cooper gave each other a worried stare. They both hated Bob because he didn't like cats and dogs, so when he comes for tea Gertrude and Cooper get kicked out the house! Cooper started growling and Gertrude started meowing really loudly.

Miss Blue then walked in and said, "I'm only joking; come on let's have a slice of cake."

Then she walked into the kitchen.

Scarlett Adams, 9 years old

There once were two animals, one a cat and the other a dog. The dog's name was Scamp and the cat's name was Bob. They lived a house with fields all around them.

Scamp and Bob lived with four servants who made sure they were fed, clean and provided cuddles on demand. Scamp was the boss. He set the daily jobs, whilst he read his newspaper and watched the news. Bob *loved* to clean (himself not the kitchen). One day, Bob was in the field and he made an astounding discovery. There was a sign which read:

THIS FIELD IS TO BE CONCRETED IN 2 DAYS TIME AT 11:00 hrs SHARP!

Bob told Scamp the shocking news. They had to think of a plan to stop it. When the servants were asleep, the animals from their village gathered in Scamp's garden. "Tomorrow, we need to meet at the field at 10:30hrs to stop this from happening," barked Scamp. Mr. Mean arrived at 11:00hrs sharp, followed by his wife. "You forgot your lunch darling," she exclaimed – but, she was suddenly stopped in her tracks by what she saw. Spelled out in rocks was the following warning:

THIS IS OUR HOME! DON'T DESTROY IT!

"Mr. Mean! Stop at once, otherwise no more special sandwiches for you!" Mrs. Mean shouted. Mr. Mean rubbed his fat tummy, looked at the field, and got in his car and drove off. Scamp and Bob were delighted! Now they could have fun in their field every day.

Patryk Niciejewsky, 9 years old

Once upon a time there was a dog and his owner Bob. They lived in a town that had mountains all around it. The cat's name was Erin. She lived with him a couple of years. They knew each other very well. Erin and Bob always went mountain climbing.

A few days ago he got a dog from his best friend. The dog was a puppy. The puppy always barked at Erin and wanted to play. It was Sunday and Erin with Bob went mountain climbing. Bob didn't take his puppy with them. He thought he was too small and weak to go mountain climbing. The puppy was left alone at home. It was a couple of hours past but they didn't come back yet.

The puppy had a very good sense of smell. He went to the mountains and started to climb. He reached the top and saw Bob and Erin. Bob had a broken leg and Erin was very tired out. The puppy ran as fast as he could and he made a loud barking sound. The people ran after the puppy because they knew he wanted to rescue someone. They reached the top and picked up Erin and Bob and took them to the hospital. Bob named the puppy Brave. They lived together forever.

Amelia Smith, 9 years old

Once upon a time there was a Kitten; she was a mischievous kitten, who runs up curtains and chews lots of cables, even at Christmas; she chewed the Christmas tree branches and the Christmas lights. Oh ho!

She is a Maine Coon who has got long, soft hair and a big puffy tail which makes you go 'a-choo'

Her name is Winter because she's pure white like snow and has big green eyes. She looks like butter wouldn't melt, but we all know the truth!

We call her mischievous Winter, because we know really how naughty she is!

Shall I introduce you to how naughty she really is? Well, she bites and nibbles anything in sight and jumps on you all through the night, but walks around so elegant and poised.

However, she's always waking grandad up with lots of noise; we are always running around and tidying up after her, but you just look at her beautiful face and she is just too cute to be mad at!

Her favourite things include being picked up by me and my brother, playing peek-a-boo and chase, and also getting her toys out of the basket.

She enjoys tormenting her sisters, Pebbles and Phoebe who are tabby cats, and often wakes them up when they are sleeping just to play.

I love my nana and grandad's cats so much, they are so cuddly and so soft to touch.

The End

Jessica Daniel, 9 years old

Once upon a time, there was a tiny little dog and an amazingly large cat. They were best friends, but one day there was a fight. Their owner had gone out shopping. They had only left one bowl of food and water so they decided to fight to see who gets the food (even though you shouldn't do that).

The cat was surprisingly large and fierce and the miniature dog was scared. The cat thought she would win undoubtedly because the dog was so tiny. So the fight initiated. It looked like the cat was going to get a victorious win, but then all the dog's friends came to help him out. They were much larger than him.

As the cat looked like she was going to back down, the dogs tipped her on to her back and they started snapping at her. She wailed, "Meow meow!"

The dog looked at her and shouted: "Stop!" So they did. "This isn't right," said the dog. "We should just share the food." And everyone acknowledged even the cat. So everyone shared the food and just at that moment, the owner came home.

"Oh my gosh," she said, "they're sharing!" and from then on they shared and lived happily ever after.

Darcy Hawes, 9 years old

The dog was called Hudson and the cat was called Coal.

They lived at Totty Hall village and this weekend was the Totty Hall village talent show which Hudson had adored since he was a puppy but Coal wasn't fussed. Hudson had been practicing his dance since he got his sparkly suit for his 3rd birthday.

The day arrived; it was the Totty Hall village talent show. Hudson's tummy was swirling all over the place and his paws were sweaty but he was still excited! It was Hudson's turn he had his stereo ready. It went black………….

He danced his heart out but everyone started to boo, laugh and make fun of him.

He felt so embarrassed and he ran back home crying with Coal chasing after him. Coal said, "Don't worry, fellow, tomorrow is the call -backs and guess what I will do it with you!''

It was the call -backs day. Coal and Hudson had their outfits ready then they got called and they started. Then the crowd went wild, people clapping and cheering and from that day forward Hudson learnt that when people are mean just ignore and try again!

THE END

Muhammed Khan, 9 years old

My Dog Cooky

Once upon a time there was a dog named Cooky and he had friends named Shooky and Chimmy and a sweet owner called Bunny until this happened. Cooky, Chimmy and Shooky and Bunny went on a mystery hunt. It was very dangerous but they had to risk it. The mission was to save Mr. P and to destroy PP instead.

They made it to the house where GP was last seen. When Cooky, Shooky and Chimmy went in, they realised that Bunny wasn't there. They thought it was exciting because they didn't like Bunny that much but until they saw a red light they weren't excited any more; they were terrified!

Cooky was really brave so he decided to go in front of the door. Shooky and Chimmy got on top of the door. After a second PP appeared and chased them. All of them ran and PP didn't know who to get. Cooky barked at her, "Ruff ruff." which meant "Get me first." but she went after Shooky but he was nowhere to be seen.

Shooky was in the basement. He found a purple key but didn't know where it goes. They almost found all of the keys – this was almost. Cooky ran to the back yard and got the grey key and before PP saw them they escaped and had a happy ending with Bunny.

Chiara Ventura, 9 years old

Hello my name is Elvis- not the singer. I am an 11 year old pug. The house I rule is great; my mum cuddles me, my dad walks me and my favourite sibling Chiara feeds me and gives me yummy treats.

Even though my house is nearly perfect, there is someone I'm not particularly bothered about. His name is Toto, the cat. Let me take you back two years ago. I was casually walking around with a belly full of chicken, when in the corner was a fluffy, grey creature. I was terrified. Little did I know he had been here for a week!

Over the past 2 years, me and Toto have our ups and downs but we have learned to like each other. We unfortunately have to share MY bed, thankfully not at the same time.

At the start of my day my dad has to drag me out of bed, so I pretend to be asleep. Once I have unfortunately had to get up, I go downstairs and look at my empty, plain food bowl. In my almost perfect house I have to walk before I eat. On the bright side the food I get is great. Chicken!

I get three walks a day and for a small, round pug I enjoy it. I do see great dogs on my walks. There is Molly a Springer Spaniel, April the Shih-tzu, George a Weimaraner and Welly a Pug!

I personally believe that I have the best life a dog could ever have and after reading my story I hope you will agree.

Alexandru Lazar

They were friends, good friends in fact. Let me tell you the story of how they met. But first let me tell you something about them. The dog is called Max and he is a Husky. The owner lost him on the streets. The cat is called Thor; it is a male. He was a cat that lived on the streets his entire life. O.K, enough with that, back to the story now.

It was a rainy day. Max was trying to find somewhere to hide from the cold and heavy rain. Then between two markets he saw it; it was a box. At first he doubted it; he thought maybe it is a trap set by the pound. But because he was cold, Max went directly to the box, where he found Thor eating. At first they looked at each other but when Thor saw that Max was lost and he had no intention whatsoever, he invited him in the box. Thor shared his food with Max. That's when I saw them. I instantly knew there was something good about them so I asked my mum if we can take them home. My mum, because she is an animal lover, of course said, "Yes."

So we got home and took care of them. Then we saw that Max had a tag on him. I asked my mum if we can keep him. She of course said, "No" and that we had to return him immediately to the owner. I was so sad. We returned them and Thor was sad too. But because he was a street cat we kept him. We keep on visiting Max, spending time with him but it is not like the old days.

Thomas Taylor, 10 years old

Once upon a time there was a dog and a cat,
They sailed around the world in a magician's hat,

First they went to France and left behind Boris,
Scored some great penalties against Hugo Lloris,

Second was Spain where there was a great disco,
They danced the night away with the fabulous Isco,

Third was Argentina a bit unnecessary,
They did a keep up challenge against Leo Messi,

Fourth was Italy where they bumped into Pellegrini,
Doing dirty tackles and being a meanie,

Fifth was Croatia where they bought a pen,
To get an autograph off the great Lovren,

Sixth was Ireland they were met by Mclean,
He said, "It's time for kick off- where have you been?"

Seventh was Germany where they got chased by a moose,
They ran off at top speed and got saved by the Reus,

Eighth was Scotland for tea with John Fleck,
They were getting worn out after their global trek,

Ninth was Wales that was not a fail,
They played a game of football with Gareth Bale,

Lastly was England the place they call home,
The cat in its basket and the dog with its bone.

Sieanna Elliott, 10 years old

Once upon a time there was a cat and a dog.... The cat (Dennis) the dog (Buddy) and his girlfriend (Puggles) lived together with their owner Carly, in a beautiful house in Sheffield. Buddy and Puggles had six puppies.

One day, Ginger (one of the puppies) disappeared. His parents looked all over the house and in the garden, but couldn't find him. Dennis the black and white cat joined the search for Ginger. He could hear snoring coming from inside the cupboard. He called the rest of the puppies, who stood on top of each other, then he leaped on top of them and opened the door with his paw.... to reveal the missing puppy. Ginger was curled up in a shopping basket, fast asleep, dreaming about digging up bones in the garden. He yawned, wondering what all the fuss was about, as his brothers and sisters bounded all over him, licking his face.

Ginger's parents, on hearing the excited puppies, ran to the cupboard to find Ginger playing with them. They licked his face, as they were so happy to have found him. The puppies told them how Dennis had heard snoring coming from the cupboard and how he had climbed on their backs to open the door.

Buddy and Puggles thanked Dennis for finding Ginger and licked their puppies. Then they all ran to the kitchen as they could hear their dinner being put out. Carly smiled at them and said, "What have you been up to?"

Isla Thompson, 10 years old

Emma lives in a parallel universe where animals live in the underworld, and humans live in the present world. Nobody knows about this except you reading this and me writing this. Maybe Emma has a hint…"Get dressed and go outside," yelled Emma's Mum up the stairs. "Bu-" Emma started to say. "No buts. You are going outside and that's final!" Emma got dressed and gloomily walked outside. Little did she know today was no ordinary day. Leaves were swirling around with the brisk autumn breeze. She didn't care much for the crisp autumn colours as she was sulking, kicking them with her red rubber hunter wellies. As she's wandering down the dusty, crooked path to the woods, in the distance she catches a glimpse of a ginger shape. All of a sudden her mind started racing: Where has it come from? What is it? Where is it going? Her steps quicken to follow it, but she is careful to keep a distance so she doesn't frighten it off. As she nears, she notices it is a stripy ginger cat with one white paw. Prowling along the tree line, it glares back at her with its glistening green eyes. Before long the cat disappears through an opening in the trees. She rushes to the opening. Kneeling down on the crunchy leaves she peers into the dark wondering where the cat had gone. Unexpectedly, out of the blue, appeared a white blur, crashing into her with its paws on her shoulders, sending her tumbling backwards. Taking a deep breath in shock, Emma sat herself up. In surprise, she saw a dirty, scruffy dog. "Sorry, I didn't see you there," said the dog. In disbelief Emma sat upright, speechless. "Hi, I'm Tom, nice to meet you and you are?" " I-I-I I'm Em-ma" she stuttered. "Where does the tunnel in the tree go?" In his rough, gruff voice he replied, "It leads underground to the animal kingdom." "What's that?" asked Emma curiously. "Come with me and I'll show you." he said tempting. "Don't be daft, I'm far too big to fit down that tiny hole." "Toss it up Ginger!" echoed Tom's voice. "Watch out!" exclaimed Ginger as a violet- coloured bottle somersaulted through the air into Tom's mouth. "Drink this, "ordered Tom. "What is it?" questioned Emma. "It makes you shrink small enough to slide down the tree hole." Excitedly, without hesitation, Emma guzzled the entire contents of the bottle before Tom could say, "Take ONLY ONE SIP…"

Harrison Royston, 10 years old

Once upon a time there was a cat and a dog. The cat was Humphrey and the dog Smudge. Their owner, Harrison, was in isolation after a flu pandemic broke out. Harrison lived in a small cottage near a river (which is where he gets his fish from) in the middle of a forest. He loved walking his dog. His cat also followed wherever they went. His cat Humphrey even helped him catch the fish.

Since being in isolation all 3 have struggled tremendously not being able to go on their daily walks or see any of their loved ones. They also struggled with lack of food as all they had to eat was fish they caught.

Harrison was thinking of different strategies on how to grow his own crops. He went rummaging through the cottage basement and stumbled across a dusty iron box. Curious as to what was inside the box, Harrison went in search for something, anything to open the box. After a frantic search, he found nothing he could use. Taking the box upstairs into the kitchen, something glistened near the window sill in the kitchen. It was just the wet fish bones Humphrey had left. Excitement filled his entire body. A lock pick, no longer fish bones!

Harrison had seen this done before on the internet; surely it couldn't be that hard. After several broken bones and many hours, he finally cracked the lock. More excitement filled him! He was saved. He had found thousands of seeds.

The End.

Lucia Leeming-Sheppard, 10 years old

There, in the dead of midnight under the glistening moonlight, stood a little stray puppy- hopelessly looking for food. A little boy came along and from that moment everything changed for this little puppy.

Soon after, that little puppy got a name! That little puppy is me. My name is Rocco. People adore me. I have a new best friend; he is called Jamie. I love him like he loves me. We both love playing ball, chase, fetch. My favourite thing of all, at the end of the day, Jamie says,"Rocco, do you want a tiny piece of cheese!" I say,"Yes."

Next door has a cat called Sheila. She is annoying. I bet she hates me. Sometimes we get along…not all the time though! Today, I was visited by another dog, called Bartahatch. He said he was a spy dog and he and his spy dog community save the world from cats terrorizing the planet. But there's no such thing as spy dogs….is there?

He took me to his dog kennel and it was amazing! There was a screen and buttons and everything you could imagine but more! Bartahatch pressed a bone and…ZOOOM!!! We were off into another world…

James Roe, 10 years old

Rover the dog lived at 12, Abbey Road and Amber the cat lived at number 16. Rover lived with the Wilham family, and Amber with the Thirnums. Amber and Rover were the best of friends. But they had an issue. At No. 14 lived Rex the bulldog. He was a ferocious dog and he hated Rover and Amber. He would not let them pass his gate. They needed a plan.

One day, Rover was looking through the hole in the garden fence, staring towards Amber's garden, when he noticed Rex, petrified of something on a petal – buzzing… Rex was scared of bees!!! Until now, Amber and Rover had thought Rex indestructible. But he had a weakness…

As luck would have it, a nest of bees had appeared in the garden of Amber's house. But there was a problem - how would Rover explain his plan to Amber? However, Rover had another friend: Sid, the pigeon. As Sid was sitting on the chimney far above, Rover called him with a bark.

"Hey, Sid!" Rover yapped.
"What's up, mate?" squawked Sid.
"Can you tell Amber my plan?"
"Sure!"

Sid took off and found Amber. He explained Rover's idea and Amber put the plan into action. She pushed the huge nest onto the Thirnums' wheelbarrow and launched it over the fence and into Rex's kennel. Rex sprinted into the Dealys' house, howling. "Serves the big bully right!" purred Amber and off she ran to play with Rover for the first time in weeks.

Jessica Booth, 10 years old

It was a chilly, dull night and no one was out in the streets at such a late hour. A little drizzle dampened the streets as a lonely, hungry thin dog roamed the narrow alleyway. Meanwhile, a small, weak cat hobbled down the same alleyway, from the opposite direction.

Both animals were unaware of each other, but were both sniffing desperately for scraps of food and a safe shelter for the night. Suddenly, face to face, they both finally noticed each other. The dog's initial thought was, "Something to chase." The cat thought, "I'd better jump high so she can't get me."

They both stared at each other blankly, but had no energy to hiss or bark, so they simply walked side by side in misery. Soon they found a cardboard box to sleep upon, but at least they had each other's warmth. They both cuddled up, the cat purring and the dog snoring.

Suddenly strange hands picked them up. Frightened and confused they were taken, but the people there kindly cleaned and fed them.

A few weeks later, both animals were feeling stronger, but they still missed each other. One day, two people came in looking for a pet and immediately fell in love with the dog.

As the dog was being taken away, she started whining and pulling towards the cat's cage. "She seems to want that cat," said the woman. "We will have them both, please."

Luna the dog and Tiffany the cat walked home happily together.

Jamie Andrews, 10 years old

Once upon a time, there was a cat and a dog called Stephanie and Jack. They were best friends and loved playing together at the park on the swings. One sunny summer day they were heading off to the park when they met Mr. Shark the professional swimmer. "Wow, are you the professional swimmer that won the competition last night?" asked Jack. "No, we were in isolation."

"Oh," replied Jack.

"Well, I was; I don't know about you, anyway."

"We need to head off now because we're going to meet our friends at the park, sorry, bye," yelled Stephanie.

"Why did you do that? I wanted to ask him some more questions."

"UUGG."

"What?"

"He wasn't real; it was a costume."

"It wasn't."

"Why did some of his nose fall off, look, it's in my hand."

"He isn't a fake. Let's go back to ask him to take off the mask."

"O.K."

"Hey, Shark, take off your mask, O.K."

"Fine, my real name is Jeff," said Jeff/shark man.

"I'm not happy you were faking but I guess we can be friends."

"Thanks, you're the best."

They became best friends and went to the park every day to meet up.

Jessica Gray, 10 years old

Once upon a time there was a cat and a dog. The cat was called Myara. She was the leader of a group of cats. The dog was called Bark. He was the leader of a group of dogs. Lassie was Bark's daughter and Trixy was Myara's daughter. The two of them were best friends which was difficult as the two groups were separated from each other and weren't allowed into each other's territory, so they found neutral ground and played there.

A farmer moved onto their neutral ground and used both the cats' and the dogs' land for his horses. They all had to move to a new piece of land that they shared but it didn't last long; they wanted to fight. Bark and his dogs barked and growled, Myara and her cats hissed and flexed their claws, then Lassie and Trixy jumped in the way and growled and hissed at their own packs.

They agreed to share the land and Myara and Bark became friends. They all lived happily ever after.

Elliott Parnham, 10 years old

At the park, Bob the dog was having fun. That was until he realised that Tat the cat was in the park. That cat was trouble.

Bob suddenly realised that the bone he was playing with had disappeared. "Where is my bone?" Bob barked. Whilst Bob was sniffing around the park for his bone, Tat seemed suspicious. "Err, I don't know anything about this bone," stuttered Tat. A bead of sweat dripped down his face and fell from his whiskers. "You seem nervous," Bob said, getting closer to the cat.

Just then Bob's owner shouted him and Tat ran off. Bob wasn't going to give up that easily and he chased Tat barking, "Give me my bone back." Tat was surprisingly fast and to Bob's surprise, Tat pounced into the back of a car and the car drove off. Bob stopped. He headed back to his owner, knowing he would never see his bone again.

Bob got into his owner's car to make their way home. As Bob looked through the wound- down window thinking what a bad day he had, another car rolled up alongside them. To Bob's amazement he saw Tat with his bone sat on the back seat. He noticed that the window on that car was also down. He felt like he had no choice. He took a deep breath and jumped.....

"Bob," shouted his owner, "what are you doing?" But before his owner could do anything more, Bob jumped back through the window with his beloved bone in his mouth. "Wow Bob, you were like a super-dog!" said his owner in shock. Bob felt like a super-dog too.

The lights turned green and off they went. Bob felt happy again.

"Until next time!" meowed Tat.

Lyra Marsh, 10 years old

The cat is a very fancy cat. She has her fur combed smartly and her collar is neatly tied around her skinny neck. She lives in an amazing manor by the seaside which is very crowded. I know. Long queues are annoying. But not for this little furball they're not. All the people in her neighbourhood love to pamper her and spoil her with all her favourite treats.

On the other hand, the dog is a very scruffy dog. He is covered in fleas and flies and mud. He lives in a dusty alley near the cat's house where everyone throws the stuff they don't want. Littering is very annoying too, right? Not for the dog. He eats all the abandoned chips and sausages and fish from the ground and licks it clean.

Once upon a time, the dog was having a walk along the seaside. Then, he saw something rather interesting. A huge crowd of people were crouching in front of something. He went to have a nosy at the strange event. But as he got closer and closer, people started to look at him and run away. As he got closer and closer, his eyes met with the cat's. He wondered why everyone was feeding the cat instead of him. Closer and closer he got, and —

REOWWWWFTZZZZZZZZZZ! (according to my expert translator, that means, 'Go away you beast'.) And after that they never saw each other again.

Scarlett Mitchell, Year 6

Once upon a time, there was a cat called Caspian, the mardy moggy, who had a household friend called Lupin. Lupin was an energetic Labrador who loved to be unconfined to chasing bees in the garden throughout the day. Lupin and Caspian both lived with their owner Blair.

A few months after adopting Lupin, Blair became poorly; the nation was at risk due to a deadly virus – COVID 19 – . This virus had killed thousands of innocent people, but Blair had mild symptoms and had to stay at home. Lupin and Caspian had to make daily trips to the shop! Lupin pushed the 'on' button on the radio before they left so Blair felt accompanied.

5 minutes into the trip: "Caspian hurry up!" puffed Lupin. "I…I can't breathe," Caspian said, breathlessly, "Can I have a kitty-back ride?"

"Eh what's one of them?" asked Lupin. Caspian climbed onto Lupin's back and they continued the trip. As they arrived at the shop, a familiar shopkeeper stood patiently waiting for the pets, holding a loaf of bread, pet food and other essentials. Lupin lifted her paw saying thank you and they set off home.

Caspian was holding the supplies in her kitty backpack. Lupin could hear sniffs... "What are you sniffing at?" she asked. "I can smell our tea!" gasped Caspian. "Don't set me off. I'm starving!" Lupin exclaimed.

After, they were treated to tea that they could smell all the way home!

Miley Sue Martin, Year 6

Once upon a time, there was a young cat named Leo who lived upstairs with his grandmother Lola. Lola used to tell scary stories about a giant scary dog who lived downstairs and made him promise never to go down there but Leo was a young curious cat.

One night when it was dark and everyone was asleep all you could hear was the dog snoring loudly. Leo crept slowly down each step and when he got to the bottom he sneaked into the kitchen to be met by a big scary -looking giant dog. His grandma was right, Leo thought. The dog was gonna eat him. He couldn't move due to fear and panic.

The dog said, " Please don't run away. I won't hurt you. My name is Beast but my friends call me B. Will you be my friend?" So Leo stayed downstairs all night talking to B and the next night and the night after that and the night after that. So they became the best of friends .

The end

Hannah Spink, 10 years old

Once upon a time there was a cat, who was a ferocious Persian with a coat as white and shiny as snow named Porsha and a dog (Pomeranian), with golden brown fur and sapphire blue eyes that twinkled like stars.

They tiptoed through the miniscule, oak door, into a land of magic and mystery…. Wonderland! They wandered for hours gazing at the many wonders stored in the forest, the golden daffodils, the blush blossom and the chirping birds. They were trying to find the palace, where the White Queen lives.

As they got closer and closer, they came across a huge obstacle. There was a deathly-deep river in their way. Suddenly, four stepping stones rose from the boggy water covered in lime green moss. They jumped onto one at a time and successfully and safely reached the other side, and there it was, the castle.

It stood tall and proud amidst the large, iron gates. However, they were courted by the guards, so they had to sneak under the gate. The pair pranced proudly towards the grand doors; it felt so unreal, like a dream, but was it just a dream?

STORIES FROM WRITERS IN THE 11-15 YEARS OLD AGE GROUP

Evie Mottershead, 11 years old

Once upon a time there was a cat called Snowy who lived with her owner Mark. He cared about Snowy lots until one day he came home with a little puppy named Marley.After that everything changed. Snowy felt like she was invisible due to her being left out and the only time she got attention was when Marley blamed her for something she didn't do. Mark spent all his spare time with Marley. Sometimes he got too carried away with Marley and he forgot to feed Snowy.

Soon enough Snowy got sick of having no attention and she decided to make a plan to get rid of Marley. First she decided to find a way to break Mark's favourite mug. Later that day Mark set off for another usual day at work but while he was busy working Snowy was busy trying to break Mark's mug. First she dropped it off his desk to make sure it was broken .She rolled Marley's toy on to it and put his toy close to make Mark think it was Marley who broke it.

When Mark got home he was furious. He put Marley in a room all by himself and kept him there for a while. Mark kept going in to give him food and water but the only time Marley came out of the room was when Mark let him go outside or go on a walk.

During that day Mark started getting closer to Snowy and he started realising how much he missed her.The next day Marley was let out of the room. Snowy and Mark got really close and they started leaving out Marley. Marley now knew what it felt like to be left out and he started feeling guilty for taking Mark away from Snowy. While Mark and Snowy were having fun together Marley sat in the corner alone and bored.

Mark saw Marley sat in the corner and realised it was unfair to leave him out. So he decided to spend quality time with Marley and Snowy. They all spent time together and they lived happy ever after.

Leila Hukin, 12 years old

Once upon a time there was a cat and a dog that were living in the pound waiting for their owners to come and get them. The owners never got along with each other and so they didn't let the dog and cat see each other. The owners were called Darcie and Simon. The owners lived next door to each other so they fought before they went to work. Darcie worked as the manager of a very big company called The Bank of Engineering and Construction® but Simon worked as the senior manager for Dye time ®. So now you know the owners, back to the pound with the cat and dog.

It was a dark sad place with many breeds of dogs. Jack Russells were the most popular breed there. There were no cats whatsoever. But you don't know how they got to the pound so let's go back to the bit before they got in the pound.

It was a beautiful Saturday afternoon and Darcie and Simon were as per usual fighting but this time they were fighting over who was better which they never did but then things got physical and the dog bit Simon and the cat scratched Darcie. Next Darcie and Simon ended up in hospital so the cat and dog were sent off to the pound.

The dog and cat could secretly talk and so the cat said, "I am so sorry for biting your owner. " The dog replied, "It's all right. I didn't mean to bite your owner," and so a few days later the dog was named by Darcie, 'Kiera' and the cat was named by Simon, 'Sammy.' The reason for them fighting over who was better was Simon loved Darcie and so they never fought no more.

The end.

Joseph Prescott, 11 years old

The Tale of The Cat, The Dog and The Snowstorm

Once upon a time there was a cat and a dog called Rolo and Coco. They lived in the remote county of Shropshire. It was the middle of winter, and an unexpected snowstorm came. At first nobody thought much about it, but when the storm's intensity rose, everyone started to panic. The snowstorm carried on getting bigger and stronger until it got so bad, the whole of Shropshire had to be evacuated. Dogs, cats, horses, chickens, everything was evacuated. Except two animals, Rolo the tortoise shell and Coco the German Shepherd. All alone in the solitary county of Shropshire, they were left by themselves for the first time by their owners Jack Pott and Hazel Nutt.

It was 6 days since Jack and Hazel went away so Rolo and Coco realized that their owners wouldn't be coming back any time soon. Luckily when their owners got evacuated, they were locked in the house, so they were surviving by eating what was in the fridge and in the cupboards.

Day 31. They were still alive but the food remaining was scarce. Every day Coco curled up around Rolo and kept her warm and alive. They couldn't survive much longer. Day 32. The snowstorm was over but so was their food supply.

Luckily, their owners came back home to a barking Coco and a meowing Rolo. After 32 days of loyalty and courage, as every fairytale goes, they lived happily ever after.

Isobel Lewington, 11 years old

Once upon a time there was a girl named Darcey who lived with her Mum and Dad. Darcey had brown hair that cascaded down her back like a running waterfall and her eyelashes feathered her green eyes like wings. Darcey was one of the many children that could not have a pet and in her case she was one of the many that loved and cared for animals.

Finn was a German Shepherd and had been in Thornberry Animal Sanctuary for 2 years. His owners had neglected him when he was just a puppy, leaving him on the streets alone. Molly was a brown and black cat, who had also been neglected and left to fend for herself. Molly had been in the sanctuary for two years.

One fateful day Darcey started to feel unwell. She had a cough and a temperature of 38°. Darcey's parents started to worry and took her to the doctors for a blood test to check if she had the coronavirus.

The results were in and now came the dreaded moment to find out if she has it. The doctors looked sad and said, "We're sorry to say this; you have coronavirus.

You need to stay at home and don't meet anyone."

Everyone was devastated.

The next day her parents came back from their weekly shop with smiles on their faces. Suddenly a dog and cat came bounding over to Darcey. Her face lit up with happiness and she began to feel better. Some might say it was a miracle but what I think it's just a bond between animal and human.

Heidi Bradshaw, 11 years old

Gizmo (my dog) and Peanut (my cat) always chewed their way through everything. One day I left for school as usual, and today Gizmo and Peanut chewed through my Xbox remote and then moved on to the wires. With a big bang and a bright flash, darkness descended on my room. After returning from school I realised my pets were missing, so I went upstairs to check if they were there, but they were nowhere to be found.

In the midst of all of this, I realised my Xbox wires were chewed up, so I turned it on to check if it still worked and to my amazement my pets were inside a game that I had never seen before. They were inside of a science lab where the professor was creating a potion, which was to be used to save the world from a deadly, unknown virus.

He attached a bottle to their collar and instructed them to save the world. Then they turned to the screen and barked continuously to prompt me to pick up the controller and finish the task. I had to guide my pets through dangerous scenarios to deliver the potion to the NHS headquarters. They were extremely grateful and with a big bang and a bright flash my pets were back at home and the health of the world population was restored.

Gabija Dubrovinaite

Once upon a time there was a cat and a dog... oh don't get me wrong, they weren't friends; they were worst enemies! Absolutely horrible!! However, one day their owners fell in romantic love, and decided to live together. Cat and dog did not in any shape or form like that idea. So they put their wrongs aside and decided to break them up. Of course like any other plan it had the bad times, with wrongs where only one pet does all the work, but they managed to work together and not get mad! Even though cat wanted to absolutely rip dog part! She didn't do it though because she misses her owner, and so did dog with his.

So after a couple of months it was Jane and Alex's anniversary (owners), so cat and dog had a brilliant plan to break them up which involves a hugeeee mess of confetti and horribly torn- apart items. It comes to around nine-ish o'clock when the two owners come back to a huge mess and they go... BALLISTIC!!!

As their eyes meet those of cat and dog, they throw them out into the cold frozen night. As they stare with a blank and heart-broken look inside they both realised that after all of these months of working together they started to develop feelings for each other. But, the sad part of those two being arch-enemies... they knew that they couldn't be anything more than enemies because they are the opposite pet gender. So they came back to hating each other after couple of weeks.

Nieve Hardwick, 11 years old

Once upon a time, there was a big, black cat and a furry, brown dog called Billy and Bob. Sadly, they lived in an animal shelter. The shelter was where they met. It was a nice place but Billy and Bob wanted a real home with humans. They looked adventurous and this was going to be a big one. On visiting day, the beasties sneaked out and went into the forest. It was a big scary place but Billy and Bob weren't afraid. They travelled far and wide, until a big truck stopped them in their path… The back of the truck was covered in big, bold letters that read 'CIRCUS'. Two men came out. They reached their hand out to stroke them. The men picked them up and into the truck. Billy thought this was going to be their new home. A few weeks passed. Billy did NOT like it! He had to learn hard tricks with a really, really loud crowd. Bob hated it too! All his nightmares clumped together: clowns, bright lights, loud music. So, they did the same thing. On transition day, the boys sneaked out again. It was not long until they wandered into a large park that said 'zoo' on the gate. Billy asked, "Why are the animals in cages?''. They soon found out why. The ferocious cats tried to bite Bob! They trotted off rather quickly to the painted dogs. Billy was shocked to see the vicious, heart pounding 'things'. This was NOT the place for them. Once again, they ran away. It took three days to find their new destination! It was quite green, big fields, lots of food; it was perfect. In the distance was a large house with flowers surrounding it. Both Billy and Bob stared at each other with delight. They waited for the owner to come.

Two hours later, two children came to the door. They had spotted the pair. The children took them inside where three adults sat. Billy and Bob both put on their 'I really want a home' faces, which really paid off. The adults agreed Billy and Bob could stay and the children screamed in excitement.

Emily Kostanjsek, 11 years old & Isabelle Kostanjsek, 12 years old

Once upon a time, the cat and the dog… Ordinary. Ordinary says everything in this morning, the same yellow and red ombrey leafs comes past the little, ginger-head, girl's window, as it does every year. But in this story it's not going to be the every year. It started when Amelia wished for a cat and a dog.

A year later.

Amelia got a rescued cat and a dog on her seventh birthday. She called them Tess and Rabi. Her parents were lucky enough to see her face light up the world and her smile to light up the universe. She started to bond with her furry friends as years went on. She now treats them like her own companions and is hearing queer whispers in her house.

One day she thought she heard something. She thought she was going mad! Then, she heard it. She peered around the corner and saw them sitting on the crisp grass, outside. Amelia bewilderedly stammered, "Yo…you talking about me?" Tess meowed, "You can hear us."

That night she laid in bed confused; she stumbled across a thought that she was magical. It must be impossible but it was true. Weeks later Amelia found herself on a mission trying to find Rabi`s owner. He is without a doubt magical just like his long-lost pet and Rabi said he was called Jock. They arrived at Scotland and Rabi was over the moon to see his owner.

They all lived happily ever after!

Harley Price, 11 years old

Once upon a time there was a cat and a dog, and they didn't like each other one bit. One day cat and dog woke up to a terrible surprise,

"Oh no, we're trapped in by the snow!" shrieked cat.

"What are we going to do?" howled dog.

"We need to dig a tunnel out," said cat.

The two of them crawled out of the window and started digging upwards. A few moments later cat exclaimed, "I can see light."

Then in unison, they scratched at the snow. In a couple of minutes they scrambled out of the hole and reached the surface. "Hurray!!" They both cheered. And they became best friends.

The end.

Ruby Hornung, 11 years old

Alone, on the snowy pavement, lay a tiny, shivering kitten with snow pouring down onto her. Across the road, meandering down the street was a Labrador with glistening, golden fur. Slowly, he approached her, picked her up gently with his mouth and proceeded to walk down the street with her.

At the back of the dog's garden was the old, wooden shed where the kitten and he now lay together calmly. Meanwhile, elsewhere in the garden, was the dog's owner who was about to clear the snow, when he heard a faint meow. Presuming it was his imagination, he went into the shed for a shovel to assist him with clearing snow. Upon entering the shed, he laid his eyes on his pet dog lying asleep with a tiny kitten!

Shouting for his family to come into the garden, he stared at the two in astonishment. When they arrived, their eyes instantly lit up at the thought of keeping the kitten. Whilst her dad refused, his daughter was insistent that they would keep the kitten (who she had already named Tiger). Within hours of Tiger and their dog being together, it became clear to everyone that the pair were inseparable. Eventually...

Dad agreed to keep Tiger and they became companions for life.

Isobel Davison, 11 years old

Their names were Matilda and Rocky. They lived in an ordinary street, in an ordinary house, with an ordinary owner. It was a normal day when their owner Betty came in with the morning post. "I'm afraid there is a change of plan today". Her eyes glinted with happiness. "I've won the best garden in Sheffield competition!" Betty then explained that she had to go to an award ceremony that night and leave them at home.

Matilda and Rocky exchanged glances. They knew what this meant. They were going to have another adventure.

Once Betty had gone, they opened the creaky oak door and in a hushed tone they started to discuss what to do. "Why don't we go and see our friends at the zoo?" suggested Rocky. "No" replied Matilda "we need something with a bit more...WOW."

"What about...." pondered Rocky "going to the moon. Yeah humans can do it so why can't we?"

They raced to The Space Centre in Leicester. They decided to use the Apollo 11. Three days later they had done it. They had landed on the moon. "YESSS" they cheered. "I know," Rocky said, "Let's put a flag up". The dog and cat made it back safely, but if you visit the moon and happen to find a spacesuit on a pole now you know why.

Freya Frost, 12 years old

Once upon a time there was a cat and a dog. Salt the dog, Pepper the cat. They spent their days playing together and getting up to mischief. Pepper had found Salt on her daily stroll. Taking the same path every day had become a chore, so she decided to change her route. It was the best decision she ever made! Trapped in a fractured fence, a wriggling figure caught her eye. It seemed to be in pain- a high pitched whine shaking its whole body. Its fur was drenched and fear filled its eyes.

Although she had no kittens herself, her motherly instinct was strong nonetheless. She picked him up by the scruff of his neck and began to carry him home. Although the path was unfamiliar her senses never failed her. Standing on the doorstep, she placed Salt down and began scratching at the door to get her owner's attention. When the door finally swung open, her mother, Melissa, let out a long sigh as she realised her cat had dragged home another rat.

She scooped Salt up, not wanting to offend Pepper. A gasp escaped her mouth as realisation hit her. It was alive! She hurried Salt inside and gathered together some towels. Melissa bathed the scrawny animal and fluffed him up. Wait... It was a pup! Through all of this Pepper never left his side. That's how Salt got his name. Salt and Pepper are meant to be together. Years later they are closer than ever.

Kezmie Gilbert, 12 years old

Once upon a time, there was a cat called Burt and a dog called Diesel. They were the best of friends and went everywhere together. However this wasn't always the case as their story didn't begin this way.

It all began back in London when Burt was roaming the streets with her companions. They were the top cats, who ruled the alleys as everyone was scared of them, even Diesel and his gang who were massive bulldogs that shared the same alley. You see the cats were clever and cunning and always out-smarted them.

Early one morning there was an almighty bang. The cats leapt from their sleep into the air with fright; the dogs darted under the nearest trash can wondering where the noise had come from. A familiar face began creeping up towards them when a memory flashed back in Diesel's head. It was the warden who took his family away when he was only a pup, and once you go into the kennels you never come out.

A tear rolled down his face with fear and pain as he watched the warden snatch Burt as he threw Burt into the wired cage. Diesel couldn't bear this, even though he didn't like Burt. He risked his life and threw himself towards the man and bit his leg, CHOMP! The cage door opened. Burt was free!

They all ran for their lives and from that day on Burt never left Diesel's side.

Evie Burgess, 13 years old

Once upon a time there was a cat and a dog. The peculiar thing about them is that they were best friends. Normally, cats are friends with cats and dogs are friends with dogs. But Ruby and Bruno were one of the best fits you could ever imagine. Each night – right before Ruby's owners would lock up the house – she would sneak out into the midst of the dark midnight to meet her non-feline friend. They would have the most spectacular time together. Bruno's owners didn't mind him running free, as he was rescued from the wild.

However, it's a completely different tale for Ruby –she lived in a wealthy household. Here she was expected to act proper and precise. Her owners never wanted a pet; they just needed one to show their high status. They hated the way cats cleaned themselves with their own tongue and despised their constant longing for being stroked. Going outside with Bruno was the only place where Ruby could be a cat... and feel loved. When they had got what they wanted, they didn't need Ruby – she had done her bit. She got cast away to the sanctuary and never saw her uptight humans again or Bruno. Abandoned.

What she didn't know is that Bruno's owners had noticed Ruby's connection with their dog and now that she had disappeared, Bruno was miserable. They knew they had to reunite them. They searched all the sanctuaries until they found Ruby. Together again. A perfect, loving family.

Brandon Kennedy, 13 years old

Spending every night in the cold and bitter alley ways of New York was a struggle. Nothing to eat but scraps that had been thrown away in the trash cans. Nothing to drink but the puddles that the pouring rain had created on the ground. No shelter and most of all no loving family to hold them tight and keep them warm. Bruce, a grey husky dog who had been a stray for most of his life and Clair, a poor defenceless kitten who had been chucked on the street.

These two animals stuck together throughout everything. True they had no owners and nothing to keep them warm or nothing to play with - but they had each other. The two animals had to put aside the stereotypical views that people had of dogs and cats at war because they had to look out for each other; one another is all that they had. Every night before they went to sleep in their carboard boxes, they would hope and pray that one day a loving human would walk by who was willing to take them in and give them a home…give them a life.

That day had come. One day a woman came across the two tiny animals and instantly fell in love with them as she picked them up and took them both home. She cleaned them up, fed them, and played with them every day. Finally, these loving creatures had got what they had always wanted…they finally had a family.

Freya Joyce Marello, 13 years old

Padding around the kitchen on his big soft paws was Bailey. Bailey was a white English Bull Terrier with the smiliest mouth ever; he also had one blue eye and one brown eye which made him even cuter! Bailey was very well looked after. He lived with his human Dorothy who was an elderly lady around 70, but she would still take Bailey for a walk every morning even in the rain.

One day, Dorothy was going to the shop to buy some bread and butter for their supper. After a while, Dorothy stepped through the door and greeted him with a rub behind his ear. Bailey followed her into the kitchen and she put a towel onto the floor with a shoebox on top. Bailey looked at her in confusion. Dorothy smiled and lifted the lid on the shoebox.

Inside the box was a small animal which had big green eyes and a big fluffy tail. Dorothy told him it was a cat called Pebbles that she had found in a shoebox by the side of the road. Bailey helped Pebbles out of the box with his nose and tried to encourage him to the living room. Bailey could sense Pebbles was nervous, so he gave him a sniff of reassurance and carried on encouraging him to the front room. They curled up and fell asleep on the mat. Years passed and Bailey and Pebbles were the best of friends, and Dorothy loved them both with all her heart.

Cerys Pratt, 13 years old

It was a beautiful day in Thornberry. Cars could be seen driving up and down the road in front of the animal sanctuary. It took a while before a car drove through to enter the sanctuary, but it happened.

The car contained a very small kitten. It had been abused and uncared for by previous owners. The kitten had a bad paw and would need a check-up before it could go with the other cats. A little bell on a collar rang next to the kitten's name tag: Hermione.

After her check-up, Hermione was put in a room with other cats. It wasn't what she was used to. All the other cats just ignored her, leaving her on her own. What she WAS used to.

One night, Hermione saw some bright lights coming from outside. Because of her size, it was easy to slip through the gates. She followed the lights straight on to the road. The sound of a motorbike came closer and closer. The headlight blinded her. She was going to be hit!

NO!

Something had picked her up and got her out of the way in time. It was Ben, a German Shepherd, that belonged to one of the nurses. Hermione rushed into the nurse's arms. That night Hermione slept in between her hero's paws. Ben had committed a noble and heroic deed and it was the least she could do.

And from that day on, the kitten and the dog became the best of friends.

Zahra Kazmi

I let these humans carry on with stressful lives they lived by taking a nap. Carefully and curiously I approached the window, staying still like a marble statue. "Is that cat real?" "Dunno. It's pretty strange." remarked the chubby man twirling a cigarette in his hand.

I'm not the ones making the earth a worse place. He could take a walk and that would help. I landed in front of the washing machine, hypnotised by it. I didn't even realise my owner call for me. "Suga? Suga come here" I heard my owner call for me. "Come here and meet Yeontan!" Who is this Yeontan? I hissed defensively and Yeontan backed away sulking. I circled my owner. She's mine. She smells like me so she's mine. "You poor thing! Come to mummy" I leaped as fast as I could.

"Not you. Come here Yeontan!" She carefully placed me down and cradled Yeontan. I just crawled away getting angry. I made my way to my owner's bedroom and scratched her pillow. It made a beautiful tear like a tiger's stripe! Maybe I should leave my scent. I vigorously rubbed myself against her bed, smiling gleefully at myself. I'm such a good boy. A good BIG boy.

She dropped the food in a state of shock. "You wretched little rascal!" Shaking her head she lifted the pillow. I just tilted my head and my pupils dilated. Yeontan silently smirked. I just meowed pitifully. I understand how humans feel but why won't they understand me?

Jess Whitaker

Once upon a time there was a skinny, battered cat and a plumpcious Labrador. Despite being a stray, the cat (whose name was Jake) had something that Belle the dog didn't have kindness.

One day, in the street, Jake met Belle. " How are you? " Jake asked Belle.

"None of your business, Smelly Cat! " snarled Belle as she snatched the sandwich that Jake had found for his tea. Poor Jake didn't know what to say.

"Belle!" Belle's owner called. Belle trotted obediently towards the owner and out of sight. That night, Jake had to go without a meal.

Fifteen days later, a kind old man named Merlin spotted Jake on the streets and when he saw that Jake didn't wear a collar, he made some Found Cat posters and stapled them everywhere. The next few days were the best days of Jake's life- he had fresh meat every day and Merlin gave him lots of love. Nobody came, so Merlin made Jake his- this meant he had to be vaccinated.

At the vets, Jake saw Belle wearing the cone of shame. She looked so sad. "Do you need help?" asked Jake. "You would do that for me?" Belle perked up. "Of course!" Jake helped Belle to pull the cone off and rivals became best friends, just by showing kindness.

Macy Boulton, 14 years old

Once upon a time, there was a cat named Tarken. He was raised in a family consisting of him and his four owners, (although calling them that is a bit of a stretch, as he undoubtedly owned them.)

Every day, he did the same things; claw his owners for food, patrol the house looking for any intruders and sneakily laying on his owners bed, even though he's forbidden...However, one day was different.

It all started on his daily patrol, when he heard a strange noise, the noise sounding similar to a dogs barking. Ears shot up, he ran to the window. It was a dog indeed! However, the strange thing is, his owners were with the dog! "This can't be right!" he thought.

The first meeting of the two was bizarre, or so Tarken thought. This intruder, who goes by the name 'Maddie', just kept barking! So he decided, being in charge of the family, he should let his owners know this is a bad creature! And the only way of doing this, is to frame her!

So he decided, he would get his Mummy's favourite shoe, bring it into the garden, and tear it up...! However, it was unsuccessful, as he tripped and landed in the pond! Oh and how Tarken detested water! He splashed and splashed but couldn't get out....

STORIES FROM WRITERS IN THE ADULTS (16+) AGE GROUP

Ben Parkin

Most days the cat and the dog would be the best of enemies. This day wasn't 'most days'. This day they were not worst enemies. This was the day when they both realised that things would be better together.

A virus had swept the animal land; dogs and cats across the land were becoming ill. Vets had never been as busy. Our cat, Jack, didn't have the opportunity to go to the vets. He was a stray cat and lived around the back of the local butchers. No one would come near Jack. They were scared of his wailing, his screeching, and the way he cried at night.

This time it was different, Jack was doing these things because he was ill. He needed help. He needed someone to come.

Days and days he would send his cry for help but no one would come to have a look round the back of the butcher.

No one would come until Joe the dog decided to build up the courage. He decided to find out what the noise was and where it was coming from. He looked high, he looked low, he looked everywhere... until he realised where it was coming from. He took a deep breath and went round the back of the butchers.

He saw Jack and their eyes locked on one another. Even though he knew dog did not like cat, he had to do something to help.

Briony Lyne

Once upon a time there was a cat and a dog,

They met when the cat was chasing a frog,

The cat, named Flora, loved to play,

She discovered a frog who was hopping away.

The frog came from the pond next door,

Flora was bold and wanted to see more,

She saw a chance and couldn't resist,

She pounced on the frog but she awkwardly missed!

The frog hopped through a crack in the gate,

Flora was impatient and she couldn't wait!

She jumped over the fence forgetting one thing,

The neighbour had a new dog and he was called King.

King was excited about his new home,

He loved the garden where he could roam.

King, asleep on the kitchen floor,

Was awakened by a noise coming from behind the door.

He looked through the glass but he couldn't see,

What was that noise? Who could it be?

His new family noticed he was beside the door,

They wondered if he wanted to go outside and explore!

King stepped out but seemed wary,

Is that a shadow? It looks scary!

The shadow moved and King started to bark,

He hadn't yet been outside in the dark.

The shadow jumped backwards and as quick as a flash,

It disappeared into the pond with a loud splash!

King bound over but who could he see?

Flora the cat looking shocked and soggy.

Flora scrambled out and when she reached the wall,

Knew the frog wasn't worth chasing

after all!

Julie Burrows

Safety in the squares

"What's happening mummy? Where are we going? I'm scared." "I don't know son; try not to worry." The people had kind voices and gave us water and took the heavy chains off our necks, so we can move and not get tangled up. The square box rattled along the road. Suddenly the rattling stopped and the box opened. There was a lot of people and voices. "Whatever you do son, stay close by my side." "I will mummy. I'm scared," he said, trembling. Mum was trembling too. She was terrified, but was trying her upmost to look brave.

They were ushered off into another square box, but this one had a big comfy bed, food hung in nets and fresh water. The voices were kind and reassuring, things like, "Hi cutie," and "Your mum's pretty" and the word "safe" kept being said. She looked at her baby and nuzzled him, and said, "I think we're going to be safe now."

One morning three weeks later, realising they go out to the big green square in the morning, and the comfy square at night, with lots of little feeds throughout, you heard, "Hey mum look! I can run, jump, spin round and do handstands (Oops didn't mean to do a roly poly). Mum, join in! Woohoo, are you happy mum?"

"Yes son, very very happy."

"Me too, woohoo!"

Holly Barlow

Ever since being a kitten, Tabby cat knew he was destined for greatness. He padded out of the apartment he lived in. "Tonight would be the night!" Confidence filled the air as he pranced down the road. He reached the wood at the foot of the estate. "No feat for me," he sneered. And it wasn't; he sneaked through it cockily. Another experience arose when he met the stream that flooded through the trees. One smooth leap saw him over the stream like it was a puddle. "No issue for a cat of my experience!" Constant feats of skill faced tabby cat throughout the night; he had no issues. "There's nothing beyond me," he boasted to his other midnight escapees. He carried on this way all night. Dawn was approaching and he wanted one final show!

"I'll climb the tallest fence around!" declared tabby cat.

Naturally, he climbed until he was at the top. A dizzying feeling suddenly flattened his head and stomach. "I don't feel too confident," he thought but was too proud to admit it. Plodding slowly round the corner was a limpy, slightly chunky chocolate Labrador. Being as kind as he was, the Lab decided he would help tabby cat. His paws grappled up the fence, serving as a bridge for tabby to clamber, quite sheepishly, down onto the ground again. Tabby cat thanked him enormously.

Rumour is they're friends to this day.

Katie Thomas

Once there was a dog named Biscuit. A happy go lucky dog. He lived with his owner, Katharine, an aspiring singer. And a darn good one too. Biscuit had a beautiful silky coat, with a golden bone tag, allowing people to have the knowledge of his name and address. He was a charmer.

Iced winds knifed people on a bitter, numbing Christmas Eve. It was a penetratingly boring atmosphere, surrounding the house where Katharine and Biscuit lived. Christmas was not their friend, as they laid lazily in the living room. "Why does everybody enjoy the company of Christmas?" Katharine asked herself. Biscuit wasn't able to reply; instead he just stared at her lovingly with his large round eyes. Katharine never understood the love at Christmas. To her it was just an excuse for greed to take over the lives of innocent civilians.

They never had a Christmas tree; neither did they have any decorations. Though Biscuit had had enough of her attitude and decided to show her the joys of Christmas. All of a sudden decorations were flying everywhere, as the dampened depressing room, suddenly transformed into the ultimate Christmas wonderland. Hours later Katharine arrived home from work, to a cheerful land of wonder and joy.

"Oh my goodness Biscuit, did you do this buddy?" Biscuit once again stared with his cute brown eyes. "Thank you Buddy, I love you mate. Merry Christmas. Now I know why everybody loves Christmas.''

Kelly Barker

Timmy was laid in the sun watching Tommy chase the fluttering things when a noise came from over the wall. Timmy looked over and he saw something in the grass. Tommy jumped on the wall to investigate. He saw a girl cat. Slowly she emerged out of the grass.

The cat saw a bowl of food and went straight to the dish. Tommy went into the house to get the attention of his human, Sarah.

Sarah was surprised to see the girl cat. Timmy and Tommy heard her say something about "kittens". She went inside. She came out with something that looked very strange, but Timmy and Tommy knew what it was it was - a beep machine. Timmy and Tommy were happy as they knew this would mean the girl cat would find its human. Unfortunately, it did not beep. Sarah picked up the girl cat and took her indoors.

About an hour later there was a sound of a van. The driver entered the house. When she came out, the girl cat was in a box. They were both confused and went inside. Sarah was on the phone saying, "Yes I know. I don't know where she came from; she had no chip. Yes, Thornberry."

With that they knew she would be safe as they had both lived there before and knew the humans there would love her just as much as their humans loved them.

Lauren Collumbine

Once upon a time, there was a cat and a dog. No, this isn't a fairytale, and no, they weren't enemies like these domesticated animals are typically stereotyped as. Their real enemy however, was man- or that is what they began to believe the day they were abandoned.

Neglected. Thrown to the side of the road: torrential rain pouring down from above started to damage their only shelter- the cardboard box which the owner discarded them in: cars whizzing past in their ignorance, disregarding every whimper and desperate cry from the animals... their insignificant presence against a harsh, detrimental world made them believe that there was no hope. They huddled together, closing their delicate, vulnerable eyes to block out the abyss before them.

Until. Something approached them. They tried relentlessly to run, but their weak legs and absence of energy meant they were unable to move- statues. They cowered, faces down towards the sludge. Their lithe bodies trembled and ribs appeared 3D through their fragile, undernourished skin. This 'something' swept them off the floor... gently though, to their surprise. Reluctantly, in trepidation, the dog and cat both opened their timid eyes...

It looked awfully like their enemy. Both animals were confused, however soon enough realised that it was here to heal not to harm, to feed not starve, to love not hate... to re-home, not abandon. These were not enemies, but heroes- heroes from the sanctuary. Rescuers, life-savers... thankful they were. Maybe humans aren't the enemy after all?

Jayne Flint

She was the wise woman of the forest; as old as the trees. Her bare feet trod softly over the canvas of the ancient woodland; those mossy pathways, those brambled passages. Sunlight scattered through the green canopy refracting an opalescent sheen that glinted off those sharp teeth. She grinned. She was wolf incarnate; the ancestral dog. Cunning, intuitive, fearless. Loyal only to those howling sisters whose mournful baying greeted her across territorial tides of the full moon.

Her smell was sharp. She felt the seasons with it; knew its cues, read the tangled hyphae of roots and fungus like tarot cards. Wild garlic lit the hum of earth like scented torches; crusts of undecomposed autumn leaves sent swirls of dust into shaded, bird-flittering air.

And then; a disruption. A girl cloaked in red picking her way through the spikes of green that would soon turn into a carpet of blucbclls. The woman paused. They circled each other warily. The girl hissed, "Get back old woman! Your eyes and ears aren't big enough to know what change has swept our nation – be gone!"

The woman growled, "But my teeth are still big enough to bite."

At that, the girl sprang like a cat, claws piercing the ancient flesh of her adversary. The woman snapped her fangs once and the girl's neck cracked like a twig.

Leah Fisher

Once upon a time there was a dog and a cat who by not fault of their own,

Ended up in a special home.

The humans were nice and treated them with care,

But something was missing, their families weren't there.

The cat was loved from being a baby,

Belly rubs, treats and cuddles with a special old lady.

However time does pass and so do we, but now the cat had nowhere to be.

The dog however never had love, and spent his time avoiding a shove.

His owners did shout, they didn't seem to care,

And the little dog didn't want to be there.

A friendly human saw his fear, and decided it was time for help to be near.

He was taken to the special home to recover from past,

And dreamt of a home where love would last.

The big day came for the little cat, who had been spotted by a lady named Pat,

She arrived at the centre to meet our cat,

She saw her blue eyes and that was that.

The love did grow, a bond began,

Between a lady called Pat and that special little cat.

The dog however waited and waited, it seems his days were definitely dated,

He watched the others find a home,

And wondered why he was still alone.

He was a good boy that needed a chance.

He was taken to a fun day for many to see,

And at last he thought this human could love me,

They came to the centre the very next day,

And took him home and by the fire he lays.

With love and affection the dog thrived,

And for the first time ever felt really alive.

Visit your rescue centre today,

They all need a home, a future and love.

Leanne Farmer

Once upon a time, there was a cat and a dog who lived together. The cat didn't much like the dog as he was smelly and loud. The dog didn't much like the cat as she was aloof and hissed at him. But one thing they had in common was their human. A girl of 6, with lots of energy and a gentle touch. She sneaked food for them under the table sometimes and read them stories. She spent hours playing with them and napped with them on her soft, comfy bed.

But sometimes it seemed the girl didn't know they were there. The dog would bark near her and she would trip over him. The cat would meow at her and she would tread on her tail. Sometimes this made the girl cry and the cat and the dog didn't know why. They didn't know that she was born deaf, and couldn't hear her friends talking to her.

But all that changed one day when a small operation gifted her with the ability to hear for the first time. Her face lit up when her beloved pets spoke to her and she heard them! Her eyes filled with happy tears as she heard the cat purr for the first time and the dog bark at her arrival home.

Yes, the cat and the dog didn't much like each other but they understood their shared love for their human.

Madison Bonsall

Blind. That's the word they used when they dropped me off there and that was all that defined me. My name's George and I'm a three-year-old black miniature Schnauzer. I'd lived in the sanctuary ever since I was eleven weeks old, but things changed there one day.

About a month ago I met Nina, a tabby cat who moved into the kennel next door to me. When Nina moved in and we began talking, I became captivated by her stories. It seemed as though she had travelled the world in just two years of her life, journeying through cities and countryside alike. Most importantly, she taught me that there was more to life than these kennels and there were amazing people in the world, like her owner Jill who had sadly passed away, hence her stay at the sanctuary. When Nina came into my life, I thought I had found complete happiness but there was so much more to come.

Now here's when my life changed forever. When a family came to adopt Nina, they were told about our bond and they decided that they couldn't possibly keep us apart. I thought I knew what life was before being adopted, but I was very wrong. Nina and my new family are teaching me about the world, and I've learned that it's an amazing place, full of happiness, positivity and most of all, love.

I belong somewhere now and there's only one word which defines me these days: loved.

Rachel Gallagher

Once upon a time there was a cat and a dog who lived in an animal sanctuary. They were the very best of friends. The other animals thought it was a little bit funny to see a cat and dog being friends, but they often played together.

One sunny day whilst playing outside, the cat and the dog noticed that all the windows of the nearby houses had rainbow paintings in them. They thought that they looked so pretty and seemed to cheer everyone up, so they decided to do their own paintings. The dog painted a picture of a small ginger cat with his tail and the cat painted a big black and white fluffy dog with her paw.

They put them in the window and then when people went for their walk they thought of all the lovely cats and dogs that are looking for their forever home and about the people who worked so hard to take care of them all.

The next day when the cat and the dog went outside to play, they saw paintings of rainbows and dogs and cats and other animals too in the windows of all the houses and schools.

They both knew as they snuggled up in the quiet of the evening, in these very different times, that no one was really alone and everybody was loved. Everything was going to be okay.

Sean Webster

A brown Boxer with black eye shadow, a vertical bleed of white foundation between the eyes spilling to the nose. 'If Scarlett's upset it can't stay.' 'May I present Johansson.' She shook her head at the ridiculous name, as Scarlett's tail went fox. They side- stepped like an awk's first date. Who's gonna get the conversation rolling? Instead, brazen Scarlett took a wash right in front of the stranger, licking and rubbing her paw over face and ears. Every evening Scarlett would nestle on her lap, Johansson at his feet.

'OMG you've got to see this!' Scarlett's favourite toy, a green and white plastic ball with silver bell inside, was rolled to Johannson. His paw whacked it, sending Scarlett scurrying again and again.

As years passed Scarlett crept slower than time, losing the love of her life, her appetite. After a home burial he was horrificd to see Johansson pedalling up the freshly dug earth. SHE MUST NOT SEE THIS. He legged it, stopping when Johannson bolted back in. The dog placed a green and white plastic ball with silver bell into its mouth and raced out. He went to intervene, but she'd seen and held his arm tight. 'Look,' she sobbed.

Johansson dropped the coloured ball into the hole. It landed with the faintest tinkle, before he pedalled the dirt back into place. That evening they reminisced. Johannson crept into the room and rested himself at her feet.

Jane Sara

Ignorance is not bliss.

'We're a nation of animal lovers,' he told his lunch guests, as his Labrador waddled heavily across the plush carpet to nudge for treats, 'and I love mine. Who else feeds their dog nothing but best sirloin, eh?'

They were distracted by an agitated cheeping from a corner of the room. A tiny bird looked out through the bars, gilded and elaborate, of a cage set on a polished table. 'Ah, my Goldfinch,' their host said. 'Rescued it from my neighbour's grotty plywood bird table last week, eating cheap bird seed. Didn't spot me with my net but look at it now - life of leisure, nothing but the best, safe from predators. Beautiful cage, too, cost a mint at Wardlow's Antiques.'

One guest started, 'But…' when a girl burst in. 'Daddy,' she wailed. 'Princess was naughty again. She wouldn't move.' She smacked the arm of the couch with a small whip in her plump fist. 'She's just lazy!' The guests followed her glare through the window onto a small paddock where they could see a lone pony almost hidden by the long, lush grass - fat, motionless, head low.

'A picture of idle luxury, eh?' he told his guests, '…but we love 'em,' he said, interrupting as the other guest began to speak.

The news at breakfast next day caught his guests' attention. It seems a local businessman had been found dead at home, throat ripped open, eyes pecked out and body trampled by something heavy.

Sophie Robinson

As his enemies approached stealthily, his heart started pounding faster. Ronny should have known by now that Rottweilers aren't allowed friends. Some kick and scream towards him, others shriek and cry and though he racked his brain, Ronny couldn't think why. Was it because he had big teeth? He only used them to chew his tea. Was it the big collar around his neck? He only had that to stop him flee. What was it that those big, scary, humans thought of to create such a vendetta against him, pondered Ronny.

But he had no time to think. His enemies kept sliding slyly towards him with that glimmer of hatred consuming their eyes that only disappeared for a blink. Just as Ronny gave up hope and cowered in the corner, something quite unthinkable happened. Hissing and scratching, a courageous cat started throwing itself at Ronny's enemies, without a thought of the consequences for itself. "Wow!" exclaimed Ronny, "I couldn't have even done that for myself". "I'm Carys, I know how hard prejudice can be. Every day I get taunted by people who don't know me. They assume I'm mean because I'm a cat, but just like you, we're not all like that!"

Feeling finally understood, Ronny smiled and gave a friendly hug. His heart slowed and grew. All of his life, Ronny had wondered why he couldn't make friends but now he finally knew - some people don't realise, no matter what dogs look like, they're just like me and you.

Kathy Hand

A Bonnie Lass

I was fat and getting up had become harder. I passed a shop window and saw a Border Collie that was fatter than me. OMG it was me! I felt sad as I ate my toast and latte for breakfast; now I know why I am fat.

I felt my people were troubled. My latest owners, and there had been a few, were taking me somewhere and I did not know where. We arrived somewhere I had never been before and there was a huge sadness in the car. I could hear lots of dogs barking but that was OK. Maybe it was a spa for my weight.

Oh no! I realised it was the RSPCA. I was to be surrendered. I knew they cared for me but had too many pets at home. They sat in the car building up the courage to take me in. Another car parked beside us and I was let out for a sniff. My owners and the couple in the car were talking then my owners flung their arms around the couple and cried. I was helped into my new people's car and off we went.

Oh no! I know that smell- The Vets!!! I had been brought for a health check.

They want to weigh me so I used my weight to my advantage and it took three to slide me across to the scales. Oh yes I was heavy- 54kgs - should be 30.

I was put on a strict diet and lots of exercise and suddenly I could get up with ease, I could chase the stick, I could swim.

Best of all for the first time I felt truly loved and cared for and that I had found my forever home. We were three BFF.

Leah Greenhalgh

Once upon a time life as we knew it changed. A deadly virus took over the world. Panic spread. After what felt like a lifetime of sleep, Stella woke. Confused, she whispers, "Hello, is anyone there?" No reply. Stella slowly clambered out of bed with a shiver as her feet touched the ice-cold floor. As Stella began to cross the room she looked out of the door and into the eerie dark hallway. Calling out again, this time louder, "Hello?" "Hi there," a voice echoed through the hall. As she shuffles towards the voice, to her surprise she sees a shadow emerge from the dark, a small form, the shape of an animal. Bright green eyes shine through the darkness. As Stella moves closer, she realises she is looking at a cat. "Oh, hello there, little kitty," said Stella. Unhappy with this statement the cat responds, "Excuse me I…" Stella screams, "AHHHHHH!" Angrily the cat says, "I am Lady Marmalade." Shocked, Stella falls to the floor. "Get up - we have work to do." Lady Marmalade drags Stella's belongings towards her and says, "Get ready, come on". Stella dresses and Lady Marmalade heads to the exit. Everything outside was green and not a person in sight. Stella asked, "What year is it? Where is everyone?" Lady Marmalade replied, "It's the year 2030. Most people died and the people who were alive left the country". Suddenly, they heard a noise in the bushes. "WOOF!" Lady Marmalade cautiously moved towards the bushes. A small puppy jumped out. Stella rushed over to the puppy, securing him and took him to her car. "He has a very sore paw; we need to take him to the sanctuary," said Lady Marmalade. They arrived at the sanctuary. Marmalade led the way whilst Stella followed with the injured pup. "How did you know he had a sore paw?" Stella asked. Lady Marmalade replied "It all began when the virus spread; I got infected and one day I was able to speak. I can understand everyone." Lady Marmalade and Stella took the puppy to the veterinary room to look at the puppy's paw. Stella notices a big thorn in the bottom of his paw. She carefully removes the thorn and cleans the area to stop infection. "He's good as new; let's get him some food," says Stella. Stella and Lady Marmalade started their new journey together at the sanctuary, helping save injured and abandoned animals.

Sue McNeela

Strains of Mary Hopkin. "Those were the days my friend, we thought they'd never end……" My Hooman pensively reminds me I'm an old cat now who's used up his nine lives. So while I soak up the window ledge sun, I dabble a paw in my pond of memories to fish out how I carelessly lost those lives.

A young, fearless me is stalking in the field. I hear Dog barking. Winding him up is my favourite pastime!

I creep from my lair and alight on his garden fence. It's only a game; there's no way he'll catch me! But as I sashay along the tightrope-narrow walkway, I spy Dog2 (fast, bouncy, never-before-encountered) launching himself towards me!

I'm scrabbling up the adjacent, towering tree to a jangling chorus of yelps and growls. But feline instinct assures me they'll back off………

"Nasa, we have a problem."

Dusk. Dog and Dog2 remain on guard despite their Hooman's frantic entreaties of, "Leave it. Get in NOW". I creep higher; Dog and Dog2 stand firm; OK, higher it is. Gusting wind. I'm almost dislodged; gouge my claws deeper into the bark; close my eyes. When I awake, darkness envelops all. No dogs to be seen, only the Hooman – anxiety personified. Hilarious! But not so much my ignominious crash landing into the field.

One down – eight to go.

My Hooman's tear-brimmed eyes caress me. "Yes, those were the days" she whispers.

Steve Hudson

They were not friends, the cat and dog, but they did lots of things together. Their best achievement ...SAVING THE WORLD.

It was a day like many others, only this day the bi-ped they lived with was distracted with urgent work and didn't notice them follow into what was usually out of bounds.

The cat strolled in, the dog sniffed and wagged excitedly. Cat took up the usual lofty position on a worktop, looking down at the excitable grinning dog. Grinning because he knew what came next. It was a game they had played before.

Flick went the cat's paw, whoosh over the side went the object, falling fast toward the waiting dog. Should it be caught or should it be left? The dog had a split second to decide. If the cat were in a good mood it could be a biscuit or some other treat. But if the cat were just a bit grumpy it could be a cup or soap or on one occasion, pepper.

Spoon! Leave it. The dog twisted and wagged, yapping for more. Cat nonchalantly flicked each deserving object. A pencil, CHOMP, a glove, CHOMP, something shiny and hard, leave. It smashed. Another shiny and another smash.

The noise alerted the bi-ped who came running, anxious and upset. "Oh no, they've smashed the petri dishes; the cultures have mixed, we've lost everything…

Just a minute though, look, joining them has killed the virus. These two have just created the antidote...the world is saved!"

Graham Bloodworth

<u>Lucy</u>

I met Lucy at a mutual friend's party. I hate them, not friends, parties. Most scientific types do. We can talk shop, by the coffee machine or canteen, but parties, our minds run along the lines of, "How much uplift is generated in a cantilevered bra, or dampening required in a Sports bra?" Don't blame me; Howard Hughes started it, designing support for Jane Russell. We end up in corners, viewing the World through complex equations. Take genetic engineering, it's become a garage piece of kit now, affordable DNA gene splitting and splicing in your own home. My speciality is, well, it's difficult to explain. Let's just say I work with animals. No, don't get the banners out. Not those sort of animal experiments. We start from new, building blocks, a genetic form of those nasty interlocking bricks that ambush bare feet. I know it's my fault but I never had a female take a real interest in my work before.

"You look as bored as I feel."

"I'm sorry?"

"Elizabeth Hunter, you are?"

"Graham Peg, Pegasus Systems. Sorry, I'm so used to being at conventions."

"Flying horses."

"Yes, we.... I design them."

"Just how much exactly, have you had to drink?"

"Only 440 ml, 3.5 units."

"Idiot."

"You said 'exactly', not me. That was unkind; it's just that I deal with numbers every day. 'Thrust to weight ratios' are important with a flying horse."

"This is a joke right? No one has seen a horse with wings."

"I have, look." I pulled up a video clip on my phone.

"That's not real; it's got to be computer generated?"

"Only one way to prove it, I have my ID card, I can show you."

That was how she ended up in my lab, looking in awe at the snow-white Pegasus, asleep in the stable box, sleek wings folded. We tiptoed out.

"When can I buy one? Name your price."

"They're not for sale."

"Rubbish, everything has a price."

"Not these, it's not a pet to trot out at Pony Club."

"What if I just walked out with it, I would make millions. You spineless man, you don't see the gold mine you have? I'm taking it. You just try and stop me, if you have the balls, because I certainly do. I grab what I want."

"Such, a shame, I thought you were, nice, had empathy. But you're just as shallow and greedy as the others."

Lifting my hand, I fired the Taser, the electrical charge causing her to spasm, fall at.... What do you care? 'Deep fake' took care to show me leaving alone in my car. No one remembered Lucy leaving, still listed as missing.

The World is not ready for my creation, Unicorns; now what would I need? Lucy, she made a lovely chestnut gelding, shame, no wings. She has a good job with the Household Cavalry, 'Trooping the Colour.' I have occasionally seen her on parade, but she never speaks.

THE END

Printed in Poland
by Amazon Fulfillment
Poland Sp. z o.o., Wrocław